G f

☑ P9-DBQ-278

He wanted to trust her, but he couldn't afford to.

He couldn't afford to trust anyone he didn't know. He had learned that to his cost a long time ago. And he hated it, being suspicious of every passing stranger. And he was attracted to Sorrel, he admitted to himself for the first time. Not just liking her or amused by her—but attracted to her. Heavens knew why, he thought wearily. She wasn't his type at all....

Emma Richmond was born during the war in north Kent, U.K., when, she says, "farms were the norm and motorways non-existent. My childhood was one of warmth and adventure. Amiable and disorganized, I'm married with three daughters, all of whom have fled the nest—probably out of exasperation! The dog stayed, reluctantly. I'm an avid reader, a compulsive writer and a besotted new granny. I love life and my world of dreams, and all I need to make things complete is a housekeeper—like, yesterday!"

Books by Emma Richmond

HARLEQUIN ROMANCE®
3609—THE BOSS'S BRIDE
3580—A HUSBAND FOR CHRISTMAS

Don't miss any of our special offers. Write to us at the following address for information on our newest releases.

Harlequin Reader Service
U.S.: 3010 Walden Ave., P.O. Box 1325, Buffalo, NY 14269
Canadian: P.O. Box 609, Fort Erie, Ont. L2A 5X3

THE RELUCTANT TYCOON

Emma Richmond

TORONTO • NEW YORK • LONDON
AMSTERDAM • PARIS • SYDNEY • HAMBURG
STOCKHOLM • ATHENS • TOKYO • MILAN • MADRID
PRAGUE • WARSAW • BUDAPEST • AUCKLAND

If you purchased this book without a cover you should be aware
that this book is stolen property. It was reported as "unsold and
destroyed" to the publisher, and neither the author nor the
publisher has received any payment for this "stripped book."

ISBN 0-373-03642-6

THE RELUCTANT TYCOON

First North American Publication 2001.

Copyright © 2000 by Emma Richmond.

All rights reserved. Except for use in any review, the reproduction or
utilization of this work in whole or in part in any form by any electronic,
mechanical or other means, now known or hereafter invented, including
xerography, photocopying and recording, or in any information storage
or retrieval system, is forbidden without the written permission of the
publisher, Harlequin Enterprises Limited, 225 Duncan Mill Road,
Don Mills, Ontario, Canada M3B 3K9.

All characters in this book have no existence outside the imagination of the
author and have no relation whatsoever to anyone bearing the same
name or names. They are not even distantly inspired by any individual
known or unknown to the author, and all incidents are pure invention.

This edition published by arrangement with Harlequin Books S.A.

® and TM are trademarks of the publisher. Trademarks indicated with
® are registered in the United States Patent and Trademark Office, the
Canadian Trade Marks Office and in other countries.

Visit us at www.eHarlequin.com

Printed in U.S.A.

CHAPTER ONE

MAD, THAT was what she was. Stark, staring, mad. She could have waited at the house. Possibly waited at the house, Sorrel mentally corrected. The woman who'd answered the door to her hadn't *actually* invited her inside. She could have asked, of course, but, no, Miss Impetuous had to see him *now*. Why? Sorrel asked herself disgustedly as she hastily side-stepped what looked like something unsavoury. She'd been searching for work for *months*; another five minutes wasn't going to make any difference. Nerves, that was what it was, which was stupid. She wasn't normally averse to confronting complete strangers—she did it all the time. It was just that his name sounded somehow—intimidating, which was daft. What was in a name? Her own was pretty bizarre and *she* wasn't intimidating. But Garde Chevenay sounded—superior. It was a French name, of course, which might have something to do with it.

Or maybe it wasn't nerves, but desperation, and she *was* becoming desperate in her search for work. Not that she must let him see that. Perhaps he would interpret her behaviour as enthusiasm. That would be good, wouldn't it? Prospective employers liked to see enthusiasm. So why hadn't he answered her letter?

Much given to mental deliberations, Sorrel trudged up the muddy slope. Tall and thin with wild curly hair that wasn't in the least improved by the misty rain that fell with such persistence, she halted a moment to catch her breath. And why was it, she wondered, that drizzle always seemed to soak you more than a downpour?

Staring round her, she surveyed the empty countryside. Not a soul to be seen. Somewhere over *there*, she'd been told with a vague point, which could, of course, mean anything.

Breasting the rise, she gave a little cry of alarm as she nearly stumbled over him. At least, she *hoped* it was him; much more of this hill-walking and she'd probably end up with pneumonia. He was lying flat, his arms inside a crack in the earth, his face in profile, and, yes, he definitely looked superior. And attractive. And young—well, younger than she'd expected, anyway. But did he look like a man who would give her a job? That was the question.

Assuming something had been lost in the hole and Mr Chevenay was trying to retrieve it, without much success by the look of things, she stated, 'I'm skinny. Perhaps I can get it, whatever it is.'

He turned his head, stared at her with eyes the colour of slate. Expressionless eyes, eyes that gave nothing away. There was an air of tense exasperation about him, which didn't bode well, and he was big, she discovered, as he got to his feet. Very big.

'Take off your coat,' he ordered peremptorily.

'What?'

'Your coat!' When she hesitated, he added tersely, 'Quickly. If he slips further, we'll have to dig out the whole hillside.' Without waiting for her to obey, he grabbed her, hauled her in front of him and began to undo her buttons.

'He?'

'A dog,' he added even more tersely as he dragged her coat off and tossed it onto the grass. Bunching her long hair in his fist, he began stuffing it into the neck of her sweater.

'A *dog* is down there?' she asked in disbelief.

He didn't bother answering—but then he didn't look like a man who was going to repeat himself. 'I'll hold your ankles.'

'Ankles?' she demanded in alarm. 'How far down is he?'

'Too far for me to reach,' he snapped as he forced her to her knees.

'Well, can't he get out by himself? Dogs usually—'

'No.'

With a little tut, she peered into the hole. All that could be seen was a very muddy rear end. An agitatedly *wriggling* rear end.

'Oh, my God,' she whispered, 'how on earth am I to—?'

'Never mind the Almighty,' he ordered, with harsh impatience, 'just grab hold of him.'

With obviously no choice in the matter, she pushed her arms in first, then eased herself into the narrow opening. She felt Garde take her ankles and

grunted in fear and pain as he yanked her upright so
that she slid more easily into the hole. Unable to see
properly, unable to tilt her head, she groped around,
felt the feather-light brush of the dog's tail against
her fingers and wriggled further inside. By touch
alone, she forced her hands to either side of his
haunches, gripped hard and, with a muffled yell, told
Garde to pull her out.

He wasn't gentle—but then, she didn't suppose he
was able to be. He grabbed her round the knees and
tried to lift, and when that didn't work grabbed her
hips, and then the waistband of her trousers and gradually eased her up. Afraid her wet hands were going
to slip on the muddy fur, she gripped harder, bit her
lip at the dog's whimper of pain, and then her body
was dropped flat on the wet earth and she was
dragged over the lip of the hole.

Her hands were ruthlessly uncurled, and she lifted
her head to see Garde hoist the little Jack Russell
into his arms and begin to check him over. 'You're
all right,' he said brusquely as he put him down. He
sounded extremely bad tempered.

Certainly the dog *looked* all right as he shook himself before scampering off, nose to the ground. Sorrel
hoped *she* was, too. It felt as though all the skin had
been torn from her chest and stomach.

'Shouldn't you call him to heel or something?' she
asked absently as she rolled onto her back and sat
up. Lifting her sweater, she stared down at herself.

'No,' he denied tersely. 'Are you hurt?'

She shook her head. There was a slight redness

across her ribs, but nothing else. Tugging down her
sweater, she stared up at him. Tall and dark with
broad shoulders, jaw unshaven and his hair wild, he
looked dangerous. *Sounded* dangerous.

'Thank you,' he added grudgingly.

'That's all right,' she said quietly. 'Being skinny
has its advantages.'

'Yes.' Moving away, he began trying to shift a
large boulder that was embedded in the earth. He
wasn't skinny. He was large and well built. Even
through his sweater she could see the bunch of his
muscles.

'Give me a hand with this, will you? I need to
block the hole before he does it again.'

Getting to her feet, she went first to retrieve her
coat, and then gave a cry of dismay at the state of
it. Forgetting for the moment that this was a prospective employer, she demanded, 'Did you *have* to
throw it in a muddy puddle?'

He didn't answer, merely continued trying to shift
the boulder by rocking it backwards and forwards.

Pulling a face, she shoved her arms into her coat
and went to help. Five minutes later they'd managed
to roll it into the hole. He then dusted off his hands,
and walked away.

'Hey! Mr Chevenay!' Hurrying to catch him up,
she added breathlessly, 'I want to talk to you.'

'I don't give interviews.'

'I didn't ask for one,' she retorted automatically,
and then halted, a little frown on her face. Was he
normally plagued by journalists? Giving interviews,

or not giving them, as the case may be, smacked of—fame. Seeing that he was now some way ahead, she ran to catch him up again. 'Are you famous?' she asked as she matched him stride for stride.

'No. Who told you where I was?'

'A woman at your house…' she began, before registering the tightening of his lips. Someone was going to be in trouble for telling her, weren't they? Damn. 'Look,' she began again, 'I only wanted to ask you something.'

'I don't do favours, either.'

'I don't *want* a favour! In fact, I'm about to do you one! Well,' she qualified, 'maybe not a *favour* exactly. I'm here about my letter. You did *get* my letter? I'm—'

'No.' He continued on towards the house.

Taken aback, because he *must* have got it, hesitating only momentarily, she sprinted after him. 'How do you know you didn't get it?' she demanded. 'You don't even know who I am! I sent it special delivery,' she continued in the face of his silence. 'You'd have to have signed for it.'

He didn't answer.

'Unless you were out when it came,' she murmured, 'and it went to the depot.' Getting absolutely no response from him, she wondered if she'd got the wrong man. He hadn't actually *said* who he was. 'You are Garde Chevenay, aren't you?'

He halted, looked at her, and then strode on.

Beginning to get cross, she grumbled, 'Well, it surely can't be a secret!'

He jumped the small ditch that divided the hill from the gravel drive—or, more accurately, what had once been a gravel drive, and was sadly now mostly devoid of its gravel and sprouting weeds—then crunched along it and round to the back of the old house.

Absolutely refusing to give up until she had a satisfactory answer, she trailed after him. 'I wrote to you about your grounds. I'm a landscape gardener,' she added for extra clarity as she followed him into what looked like a utility room. 'So you see—'

'You're going somewhere?' he enquired with hateful interest.

'Yes,' she agreed firmly, 'I'm going to tell you what I can do.'

'I wasn't aware I'd shown any interest.'

'You haven't. Yet. But, Garde—'

'Mr Chevenay, to you, and don't tramp that mud in here,' he ordered disagreeably.

'You are,' she pointed out.

'I live here.'

With a little tut, Sorrel kicked off her ruined shoes and padded after him in her socks—wet socks—and bumped into his back as he suddenly halted to remove his own boots.

'Sorry,' she muttered.

He said something she didn't catch, dragged off his wet sweater, tossed it aimlessly towards the corner, and opened the door in front of him. Striding through, rolling up his shirtsleeves as he went, he left it to swing shut behind him.

'You are so *rude*!' she complained as she yanked it open and followed him along a stone-flagged floor the colour of chestnuts.

'Possibly because I didn't invite you.'

'But you must be *interested*! Your gardens are an absolute mess.' Halting in pleased surprise, she stared curiously round her at white walls, a few highly polished pieces of furniture. Stark. Monastic—which was appropriate, seeing as it was an old monastery. A beautiful old staircase ran up the outside wall; a small half-moon table stood between it and the double front doors that were curved at the top. There was one door to her right, beneath the rise of the staircase, and three on her left. There was an empty niche between the first two doors and an old table beneath. 'This is so nice—' she began.

'I'm glad you approve,' he derided sarcastically.

With a little twitch of her lips, she halted before a large tapestry that hung above an old carved chest in the space between the next two doors. 'A bit shabby,' she added sadly, 'but then it is rather old, I expect.' When there was no answer, she looked round to find herself alone. The only indication of where he had gone was the muffled click of the door at the end. Hurrying towards it, she shoved it open and went into what was clearly his study. A very state-of-the-art study. Very modern, very functional, with, as far as she could see, every technological aid that had ever been invented.

'I gather you work from home,' she murmured as she continued to look round her.

He didn't answer, merely seated himself behind a massive desk. But then he would need a massive desk; he was a massive man. It was nice to meet someone taller than herself.

Abandoning her evaluation of the room, she reverted to the subject in hand. 'So, did you really not get my letter?'

'I don't read unsolicited mail.'

'Not even out of *curiosity*?' she asked in astonishment.

'No.' Linking his hands on the paper-strewn desk, he looked her up and down in a rather rude appraisal.

She stared back with humorous defiance. She knew exactly what he saw. A stork. Too tall, too thin; her strange-coloured hair would be even wilder than usual because it was wet. Even damp, it went into tight, impossible-to-comb curls. Her eyes were too light, lashes too dark, and her nose was probably red. Fine-featured, she wasn't pretty but, at first glance, she was rather startling. She did *not* look like a gardener. Her eyes still alight with amusement, she headed for the linen-covered chair in the corner.

'I do hope you aren't intending to sit down in that muddy coat,' he stated without inflexion.

'And who made it muddy?' she asked lightly as she removed it, looked around for somewhere to put it and, finding nowhere, folded it inside out and put it on the floor. As she sat down she curled her feet beneath her and stared at him once more. 'Are you always this bad tempered?' she asked curiously.

'Yes, and only beautiful women can get away with being outrageous.'

'Rubbish,' she said dismissively. 'Anyone can get away with being outrageous. People are so astonished at your crass cheek that they let you get away with it. And if you think *this* is outrageous, you should see me when—'

'No, thank you,' he interrupted. Holding out his hand, he waited.

She stared at his hand, then back to his face.

'You have a copy of this letter?'

'Well, of course I don't have a copy!' she denied in exasperation. 'Why would I? It doesn't work like that. I write, you respond...'

'But, I didn't.'

'Well, no, but—'

'There aren't any buts. Why did you come?' he asked bluntly.

Because I was desperate. But she couldn't say that, could she? No. 'I was in the area,' she lied glibly. Still staring at him, examining his harsh, rather square-cut face, and those slate-grey, expressionless eyes, she said hopefully, 'Coffee would be nice.'

'I dare say it would, Miss...?'

'James. Sorrel James.' Her lips twitched slightly at the expression on his face. 'Daft, isn't it? But my mother was into horses at the time and I was born with brownish-orange hair.'

'It's still brownish-orange,' he commented.

'Yes,' she agreed, 'and I don't know how you have the cheek to sneer at my name when yours is even more bizarre. At least people have *heard* of Sorrel. I mean, Garde isn't exactly run-of-the-mill, is it? A family name?'

'No, and I have no idea what my mother was into,' he returned rudely, throwing her own words back at her.

She grinned. 'Coffee?'

He stared at her for a moment. Genuine, or ingenious? he wondered. It might be interesting to find out exactly *what* little game she was playing. He depressed a button on the intercom. There was a faint squawk and he said quietly, his gaze still on Sorrel, 'Coffee for two, please, Mrs Davies.' Still watching her, he asked, 'Why were you in the area?'

Lowering her lashes, she scratched absently at the mud on the knee of her trousers. Don't tell lies, Sorrel. Tell the truth. 'Actually, that was a lie,' she confessed. 'I drove down to see you.' Looking up, she stared at him once more. 'I want to do your gardens. I'm a lot stronger than I look,' she promised in the face of his obvious scepticism. 'And I'm very good. You won't be disappointed.'

'Won't I?' he asked flatly.

'No.'

'And do you normally seek people out? Knock on their doors?'

'Sometimes,' she admitted quietly.

'How many times? Come in,' he called when there was a faint tap at the door.

A rather worried-looking woman in her early fifties entered, carrying a tray. It was the woman who had answered the door to her earlier. She smiled rather nervously at Garde, gave Sorrel a curious glance and put the coffee on the corner of the desk.

'Thank you, Mrs Davies—and, in future,' he added in a voice that was guaranteed to terrify a timid heart, 'if anyone else calls, I'm not in. Neither do you know where I am, or what I'm doing. Is that clear?'

'Yes, sir.'

'It wasn't her fault,' Sorrel put in quickly, with a sympathetic smile for the other woman. 'I told her I was an old friend.'

Eyes still on Mrs Davies, he said, 'The same applies to old friends. Take their name and a contact number or address.'

'Yes,' she whispered. 'Sorry.' She gave another nervous smile and went out, closing the door softly behind her.

'Bit harsh, weren't you?'

He didn't answer, merely waved his hand towards the tray, which Sorrel assumed meant she was to pour, and with a rather wry smile she got to her feet. 'How do you take yours?'

'Black.'

'Figures.'

She poured his, then her own, adding a generous amount of cream and sugar, and then returned to her chair and stared at him. 'You seem rather paranoid about your privacy,' she commented. When he didn't answer, merely returned her stare, she continued,

'Because   you're—what?   Famous?   Wealthy?
Important?'

'No. How many times?' he repeated.

With a comical little grimace, she confessed,
'Well, none, actually. This is the first time.'

He looked as though he might believe it. She
didn't know *why* he might believe that, but...

'How did you find me?'

'Find you?' she echoed. 'You make it sound as
though I was looking.' Suddenly remembering his
earlier comments, she added thoughtfully, 'Up on the
hill, you said you didn't give interviews, as though
I might be a reporter.'

He waited, and she gave a small smile. She was
actually beginning to like this rather abrupt man, and
she gave a soft, infectious laugh. 'I found you at the
dentist,' she finally explained. 'I was waiting, as one
does, and leafing through a magazine, and there you
were. Garde Chevenay, the new owner of
Blakeborough Abbey. There was an aerial view of
the grounds, and I yearned to do them,' she said simply. 'I did have a quick peep at the rear,' she confessed. 'That old paving needs some attention—but
if you didn't want or couldn't afford to have the
whole thing done at once,' she added quickly, 'I
could do it piecemeal. Or even just the gravel. I'm
very good at gravel.'

'You do surprise me,' he said sardonically. 'The
dentist is local?'

'What? Oh, no,' she admitted with a small grin.
'London. I don't have much work on at present.'

'And one must grasp at opportunities as they arise?'

'Yes, so you see…'

'You have proof of your identity?' he interrupted.

Puzzled, she shook her head. 'Not with me, no. Why?'

'Because I want to know who you are.'

'But you know who I am. I just told you.'

'Did you?'

Slightly bewildered, she nodded. 'Yes.'

'But you didn't bring identification?' he asked with drawled sarcasm. 'Not very professional.'

'No—I mean—yes.' Taking a deep breath, she stated positively, 'I brought my portfolio.' Leaping to her feet, she said eagerly, 'I'll go and get it. It's in my truck. Then you'll be able to see what I can do…' Before he could comment, she hurried out, walked gingerly across the gravel in her socks and collected it. Hurrying back, she laid it on the desk before him. 'My card's inside the front cover.'

He nodded and opened the photograph album. Pulling a piece of paper towards him, he jotted down her name and address and then closed it.

Watching him, she felt her eagerness begin to dissipate. 'Aren't you going to look at the photographs?'

'No,' he said dismissively.

'Then why did you want it?'

'So that I can check you out.' Picking up the album, he tried to hand it to her.

She put her hands behind her back. 'I'll leave it

with you. I can pick it up tomorrow. You never know, you might find some of the ideas useful...'

'No,' he said softly.

'Yes. And if you really don't—'

'I don't.'

'You could post it back to me.'

'It might get lost,' he said blandly.

'I'll take that chance. Please? I really am very good.'

'And cheap?' he asked interestedly.

'Well, no, but...'

Eyes holding hers, he dismissed her softly. 'Good-bye, Miss James.'

With a little grimace, she quickly finished her coffee and picked up her coat. 'At least *look* at them,' she pleaded. 'I'm open to suggestions...' Realising what she had said, she gave a grunt of laughter. 'Not *those* sort of suggestions, I just meant—'

'I know what you meant.'

Pulling a face at him, she slung her muddy coat round her shoulders. 'I'll see you tomorrow.'

Not if I see you first, hung in the air between them, and she gave a rueful smile. After opening the door, she returned for the tray. 'I'll take it back to the kitchen, shall I?'

'It won't do you any good.'

'That wasn't why I... Sorry, I tend to get a bit—'

'Carried away?' He was staring at her with an expression of such *interested* attentiveness that she laughed.

'All right, I'm going.' Don't push your luck,

Sorrel, she warned herself. Hastily escaping, she awkwardly closed the door behind her. She knew she did *tend* to get a bit carried away in other people's houses, but then that was probably because she usually *worked* in other people's houses. And he hadn't *forced* her to take back the portfolio, so there was still hope, wasn't there? Ever the optimist, smile still in place, she headed down the hall.

Assuming that kitchens were normally at the rear of a property, she pushed open the door beneath the staircase, and came to an abrupt halt. The room looked like something from the Middle Ages, and the contrast with the hall was—well, astonishing.

Mrs Davies was sitting at the long scrubbed table in the centre of the room. She looked as though she'd been crying. Putting down the tray, Sorrel asked gently, 'Are you all right?'

'Yes. No. I don't know what I'm supposed to be *doing*!' the housekeeper exclaimed. 'He doesn't *say*! Mr Craddock, the last owner, was so—easy.' Staring at Sorrel, she burst out, 'I *need* this job. Clive's out of work at present—my husband,' she explained, 'and although Mr Chevenay said I could stay on, I don't know what he expects of me.'

'Because he doesn't say,' Sorrel agreed sympathetically. 'I'm sorry I got you into trouble.'

'It wasn't your fault, not really. Could you ask him?' she pleaded. 'What my duties are?'

'Me?' Sorrel exclaimed in astonishment. 'But I don't know him! I'm not really a friend...'

'Please? If I Hoover, he asks me to stop; if I cook

him meals, he doesn't eat them. I don't even know if I'm supposed to answer his phone! And now he wants me to redesign his kitchen! I know it's a bit old-fashioned, but redesign it *how*?'

'Get some magazines,' Sorrel advised. 'That's what people normally do, isn't it? Show him some pictures. And surely it will be better for you to work somewhere, well, modern?'

'I suppose,' Mrs Davies agreed gloomily. 'If I'm here that long. I don't think he even likes me. I've asked him and asked him to call me Davey, like Mr Craddock used to, but he won't. Mrs *Davies*, he says. So—so *polite*!'

With a little grin, and because Sorrel knew exactly what she meant and what it was like to have no job, no money, Sorrel agreed. 'All right, I'll ask him.'

'Thank you,' Mrs Davies said gratefully. 'You must think me an absolute moron, but…I'm not *usually* like this,' she confessed. 'Or, I wasn't. Perhaps it's the menopause.'

'Oh, dear,' Sorrel murmured.

'Yes. I keep getting hot.' Mrs Davies sighed. 'And he makes me so flustered. He's so—well, angry-looking, isn't he?'

Was he? Yes, Sorrel supposed he was.

'And his voice is so…'

'Derogatory?' Sorrel offered, tongue in cheek.

'Yes, as though he doesn't have a very high opinion of anyone.'

'Perhaps he doesn't,' Sorrel murmured. It was something she could well believe.

'He makes me feel stupid,' Mrs Davies continued, 'and although I'm not very clever I *can* cook and clean and everything. I worked for Mr Craddock without any trouble. I wish he hadn't left.'

'Well, look on it as a challenge,' Sorrel said bracingly. 'You'll soon get used to him, I'm su—'

'And now, with the reporters and everything,' Mrs Davies continued, as though she hadn't heard, 'I just don't know what to do.'

'The reporters?'

'Yes. They all seem to hate him.'

Astonished, Sorrel just stared at her. 'Why on earth would they hate him?'

'Oh, I don't know,' Mrs Davies said wearily. Getting to her feet, she carried the tray over to the sink.

Staring at the housekeeper's bent back, Sorrel asked hesitantly, 'Is he famous?'

'Famous? I don't know. All I do know is that every time I go out I fall over the reporters clustering at the gate. I'm not allowed to talk to them,' she added crossly, as though that were yet another bone of contention between them.

About to ask for clarification, Sorrel suddenly caught sight of herself in the mirror above the sink. Diverted, she stared at her image in astonishment. 'Good grief,' she whispered. 'I didn't know I looked that bad.' Her face was *filthy*! And her hair, still tucked into the neck of her sweater, was liberally decorated with mud and grass. Untucking her hair and brushing off the worst of the debris, she scrabbled in her pocket for a tissue. Peering into the mirror, she began to clean herself up. 'Not perfect,' she sighed, 'but better than it was. Oh, well.' With a crooked smile at Mrs Davies and a little shake of her head, she walked across to the door. 'I'd better be off.'

'You won't forget to ask—' Mrs Davies began urgently.

'No, no, don't worry.'

'Now?' she asked hopefully.

'Now?' Sorrel queried in alarm. She didn't think *now* was a very good idea.

'Please?'

Too soft-hearted by far, Sorrel reluctantly agreed. 'Oh, OK, but I can't promise anything.'

Walking back to the study, she gave a brave little tap on the door, and quickly put her head inside. 'Sorry to interrupt,' she began.

He looked up from her open portfolio, which he'd obviously been perusing, and asked derisively, 'Back again so soon, Miss James?'

'Mmm,' she agreed ruefully. 'There was just one thing...'

'I thought there might be.'

She widened her eyes at him. 'You're barking up the wrong tree,' she told him softly. 'It's about Mrs Davies. You seem to have frightened the poor woman to death. Not intentionally, I'm sure,' she added quickly. 'But if you could just tell her what her duties are, when she's to Hoover, cook, etc...'

'Thank you,' he said without inflexion. 'I'll be sure to do so.'

'Good.' With a little grin, she added reprovingly, 'And you might have told me I had a muddy face.'

'Why?'

'*Why?*' she exclaimed. 'Because…'

'Go *away*,' he ordered softly.

Grin widening, she put her coat more securely round her shoulders and walked out. She closed the door very softly behind her. And then she laughed. 'Yes!' she whispered with a little clenched fist. If he'd been looking at her work then he wasn't *totally* disinterested, was he? And if she didn't get the job, well, she was still rather glad she'd come. She'd really rather liked him. And it would be someone to dream about, wouldn't it?

Staring at the closed door, Garde gave a brief grunt of laughter. This procession of 'wannabes' was getting more bizarre by the minute. He didn't think he had ever met anyone so—well—ingenious, he supposed. He'd have liked her to be genuine, but he very much doubted she was. How on earth had they managed to recruit a gardener? If she was indeed a gardener. He should never have let her in the house, of course. Wasn't even sure why he had. And tomorrow she would be back. The so-very-different Miss James. And after Miss James there would be someone else wanting to do his garden, or clean his car, sweep the chimneys… Their inventiveness was endless. But, he suddenly thought, if he employed Miss James, the hassle might stop for a while, mightn't it?

With a small, rather cynical smile, he thoughtfully moved his gaze back to the portfolio. His garden did *need* doing; maybe he could kill two birds with one stone. And if she was no good, then she wouldn't get paid.

Turning back to the front page where her card was sellotaped, he decisively pulled the telephone towards him and punched out the number of a private detective.

Poking her head into the kitchen, Sorrel assured the housekeeper that she thought Mr Chevenay would be far more reasonable in future, and went to retrieve her shoes.

Crunching round to the front, she stared at the lowering sky. June was supposed to be flaming, not this perpetual drizzle. It was also the time of year when people were supposed to feel more cheerful. But not in this house. And not in the local press either, according to Mrs Davies. So why would a young man be hated? Well, not *young* young, she mentally corrected. She would guess that Garde Chevenay was in his mid- to late thirties. And extraordinarily attractive, despite his rather brusque manner. Or maybe even because of it. But hated?

Climbing into her old truck, and praying it would start the first time, she twisted the ignition key. Garde Chevenay. Definitely a name to conjure with. It seemed a long time since she'd had a light flirtation with an attractive man, and the thought of it definitely made her feel brighter. Not that she expected him to reciprocate, but it could be fun to tease him. *If* he would allow her to do his gardens, which she very much doubted.

Bit of a wild goose chase, really, which was a pity, because the front certainly needed attention. The grass, which had once, presumably, been a lawn, was waist-high and full of weeds. The trees, old and bent, were in dire need of pruning, or even removing. The drive needed attention, the stream that ran along the foot of the property needed clearing out, and the brief glimpse she'd had of the back, well... In your dreams, Sorrel, she sighed to herself. Even if he were interested, she had no references to prove her trustworthiness, and Garde Chevenay definitely looked like a man who would want references. Just like the others before him. The worrying thing was, she'd never *needed* references until after Nick. She'd always got her work by word of mouth; but now, suddenly, everyone wanted a reference from her last employer.

With a smile equally as cynical as Garde's, she sighed. That was really likely, wasn't it? A reference from Nick. And it had to *be* him behind it all. She'd had several enquiries from her advertisements, had given quotes, and everything had seemed fine—until the excuses started coming in. 'Not quite what we want. Sorry.' 'Too expensive.' 'Too this, too that, and, of course, without a reference from your last

employer...' 'One has to be so careful nowadays...'
And if she didn't find a job *soon*...

Feeling despondent again, she drove to a small hotel where she would book in for the night. She went up to her room. She would ring her sister to see if she'd managed to get hold of that article Sorrel had started reading in the dentist's, and even if she hadn't she might have been able to find out something else about him, something that might give her a lever in persuading him that he needed her. Jen liked a challenge. They both did. Oh, do stop it, she scolded herself. Things would get better. They *had* to.

Making herself comfortable on the bed, she picked up the phone and punched out her sister's number. It was answered on the second ring.

'Jen?'

'Sorrel! Where on earth have you *been*? I've been trying to get hold of you all day!'

'Have you?' Sorrel asked in alarm. 'Why? Has something happened?'

'What? No! Are you at home?'

'No, Wiltshire.'

'Wiltshire?' Jen exclaimed. 'What on earth...? No,' she said disgustedly, 'don't tell me. *That's* why you wanted me to find the article, isn't it? You went to see him! I don't *believe* you, Sorrel! You can't just go knocking on people's doors!'

'Of course I can,' Sorrel argued softly. Easily conjuring up an image of Garde's face, she smiled to herself. 'You can meet the most delightful people.'

There was a little silence, and then Jen reproved

meaningfully, 'I don't like the way you said that. What's happened?'

'Nothing.'

'Sorrel,' Jen warned, 'you know I'll get it out of you in the end so you might as well tell me now. What *happened*?'

'*Nothing* happened!' Her eyes lit up with sudden laughter. 'I just found him—interesting,' she murmured softly.

Her sister gave a snort of disgust. 'Well, don't get *too* interested,' she cautioned brusquely.

'Why not?' Sorrel grinned. 'I haven't had a decent flirtation in *ages*!'

'Because he's dying!'

CHAPTER TWO

HER mind suddenly blank, her whole body empty, Sorrel whispered in shock, 'Dying? But he can't be. He looks so healthy.'

'Well, that's what it says in the article I found. The one you didn't have time to finish reading at the dentist's. Hang on a minute and I'll read it to you.' There was a momentary silence at the other end, followed by the rustling of pages and then Jen's voice again. 'Er, blah, blah, blah. Oh, yes, here we are. At the end of the article it says—although I have to admit it's a rather odd statement,' she commented with brief puzzlement. 'It mentions some of his business dealings and that he's recently sold off his finance company to the Americans, and, bearing in mind,' she added, 'that the article is over six months old, it then says that perhaps it's not surprising he's so successful as he's riven by cancer.'

'Cancer?' Sorrel echoed, and the alarm and pity she felt seemed out of all proportion to the fact that she barely knew him. 'Are you sure that's what it says?'

'Of course I'm sure!'

'But it doesn't make sense!'

'Well, no, but that's what it says.' There was another small silence, and then Jen stated in what sounded like exasperation, 'You liked him.'

'Yes, I did, but please, please, don't tell me that I have screwed judgement, that I—'

'But you do.'

'Not always,' she defended.

'Yes, Sorrel, always!' Jen insisted.

'But Garde's not in the least like Nick,' Sorrel protested. 'You begin to make me feel as though I should suspect everyone!'

'Not everyone.' Jen sighed. 'It's just that—well, I *worry* about you, Sorrel. Go on, then, tell me about him!'

'You don't need to say it like that! He really isn't in the least like Nick.'

'Then what is he like?'

'Oh, large, abrupt, derisive. Quite rude, in fact.'

'And you *liked* him?'

'Yes,' she agreed defiantly. 'He was—different. And I can't *believe* he's ill! He looks so disgustingly well!'

'Perhaps he's in remission,' Jen murmured. 'Is he going to let you do his gardens?'

'I don't know. I'm to see him again in the morning.'

'But why go all the way to *Wiltshire*?' Jen demanded worriedly.

'Because I didn't think Nick would have any influence down here!' Sorrel stated crossly. 'And the girl I was covering for at the garden centre is coming back on Monday,' she added gloomily.

'Oh, hell, I'd hoped she wasn't coming back.'

'So did I.'

'Oh, darling, I'm so sorry. Does the job look hopeful? Although, if he's dying,' Jen murmured worriedly, 'it's probably best not to get involved. I couldn't bear for you to be hurt again.'

'I'm not intending to get involved! All I said was that I found him interesting!' Anyway, even if she'd wanted to, which she didn't, there probably wasn't going to be an opportunity *to* get involved. Sorrel quickly changed the subject. She didn't want to discuss Garde further, she found. Not even with her sister. 'How's my nephew?'

'In disgrace!' Jen laughed, but Sorrel could still hear the underlying worry in her sister's voice. 'He pulled the wallpaper off the wall behind his cot and when I told him off, the little wretch just looked at me with his big blue eyes and said softly, "Oh, dear."'

Sorrel laughed. 'I seem to remember someone else doing that. Must run in the family.'

'The difference being I got a smack!'

'Mmm, I remember.'

'When are you coming home?'

'Oh, tomorrow, I expect. Give my love to the naughty one, and to your delightful husband. I should be back about five—and I'm all right. Really,' she insisted. 'Take care of yourself. Bye.'

Slowly replacing the receiver, she continued to stare at it for a few minutes. She didn't want him to be ill. She couldn't believe he was. But was that why he'd said he didn't give interviews? Possibly. Once the article had come out... Anyway, she wasn't likely to see him again after tomorrow.

Sorrel tried to stop thinking about it, about him. She swung her legs to the floor and went to have a shower and wash her hair before going down for something to eat. But her mind wouldn't leave it alone. All that evening and long into the night she continued to think about him, and the next morning, driving out to the house, she continued to think about it.

He must have been watching for her, or maybe it was coincidence, but he answered the door himself before she even had a chance to tug at the old bell-pull. Then she realised that it wasn't either of those things as the little dog they'd rescued the day before trotted out.

'He got home all right, then,' she murmured inanely.

'One can only assume so.' At her look of astonishment, he added brusquely, 'He isn't mine.'

'Oh.'

'He visits.'

'Oh,' she said again. 'Have you, er, had a chance to look at the photographs?'

'Yes. You'd better come in.' Holding the door wide, he waited for her to step inside and then closed the door behind her and led the way to the study. He was having second thoughts about this. Overnight, he'd almost convinced himself that she'd looked calculating. But she didn't. She looked almost as eager as the damned dog. She also looked surprised, as though she'd expected him to hand the portfolio back at the door.

Moving to sit behind the desk, he looked down at the album that lay in front of him. There was still time to change his mind. He glanced at her, trying, perhaps, to analyse a face that defied analysis, then returned his attention to the album.

'Did you find anything you liked?' she asked eagerly. Moving to stand beside him, she flipped over the cover. 'They all show before and after...'

He stared at her.

'Sorry,' she mumbled, her face rueful.

'Sit,' he ordered.

Obediently turning away, she walked to sit in the chair she'd used previously. Her eyes on his strong face as he flipped the cover closed and began tapping a fingernail on it, she tried to see signs of illness, and couldn't. He didn't look thin, or pale, and certainly his hair wasn't falling out—but then perhaps he hadn't had chemotherapy. Or maybe it had grown again. Maybe he was now better. Jen had said that the article was over six months old. Certainly he looked really rather—well, rugged, she supposed. He was freshly shaven, and wearing an expensive-looking light grey, short-sleeved shirt with his long legs encased in clean jeans. There was an aura of strength, determination about him. No way did he look like a man who was dying.

The phone rang, and she gave a little start. Garde ignored it; when she couldn't bear the intrusive ring any longer, she demanded, 'Aren't you going to answer it?'

'No.'

'Well, don't you have an answering machine? Surely all this equipment isn't just for show?'

He ignored her. The phone, thankfully, finally stopped ringing.

'Did you see the letters of—well, praise, I suppose you could say, in the rear pocket?' she asked him. Best to mention them and perhaps, hopefully, he wouldn't notice that the last one was more than a year old.

He didn't answer, but then he didn't seem to answer anything he didn't want to, including his phone. It seemed a funny way to run a business. If he had a business. She should have paid more attention to what Jen had been saying.

Holding his eyes for long, long moments, unsure of what message, if any, he was sending, she rushed into speech. 'I rang my sister last night, to tell her about you. I'd asked her to try and get hold of the magazine I didn't have time to finish reading in the dentist's. It said you had cancer,' she blurted.

Amazingly, he laughed. Derisively, admittedly, but still a laugh. 'And that accounts for your worried air this morning?' he mocked.

'Yes,' she agreed. 'I was awake half the night thinking about it. I'm so sorry.'

'No need to be,' he said with an indifference that startled her. 'It was a misprint.'

'Misprint?'

'Yes. It should have said I was *driven* by Cancer, the birth sign, not riven by it. The reporter was obviously into horoscopes. The printer or typesetter wasn't.'

'Oh,' she commented inadequately, and then she smiled in relief. 'I'm so glad.'

'So am I,' he agreed drily.

'I didn't *think* it made sense! It said you were successful.'

'Did it?' he asked with even more indifference.

'Yes.' Hiding a smile, watching his large, capable hands as he moved the album and began squaring papers on his desk, she felt comforted. Turning her attention to his profile, she decided that she liked very much what she saw. A strong, well-sculpted face. A man who made decisions and stuck to them. Perhaps. A man not given to small talk. A man who didn't cheat? Someone who was perhaps slightly intimidating to anyone other than Sorrel—who was rarely intimidated by anyone.

'Who took the photographs?' he suddenly asked.

'I did.'

He nodded.

'You don't believe I'm a landscape gardener, do you?' she asked quietly. She'd often had this rather dubious response before.

'I believe you know about gardens,' he qualified.

With a little frown on her face, remembering his almost paranoia about secrecy the day before, she continued, 'You don't think I did the gardens in the photographs?'

'Did you?'

'Yes. Yesterday,' she added thoughtfully, 'and even now, you seem to be implying that I might be something else. Is that it?' Had Nick got to him? Had he somehow found out she was coming down here? No, he couldn't have done. So why was Garde Chevenay being so suspicious? 'I don't understand why you seem to suspect me of ulterior motives.'

'Your behaviour?' he prompted.

'But I'm always like this. Or do you mean because I turned up so unexpectedly? But that was because—'

'I didn't answer your letter—yes, you said.'

'And I'm sure you're quite capable of snubbing any pretensions I might have, if that's what's worrying you.'

'It isn't. Do you?' he asked drily. 'Have pretensions?'

'No,' she denied slowly and really rather worriedly. She had never thought she looked like a person on the make, and yet, this last year...

'And now?' he asked.

'Now?' she echoed in confusion.

'Yes. What will you do now, Miss James?'

So he didn't want her, she thought despondently. Why invite her in, then? Why prolong the agony? 'Nothing,' she said. 'If you don't want me to do your gardens, I go away, back where I came from.'

'To do what?'

Wavering between honesty and pride, she stated almost defiantly, 'Whatever I can. I've been helping out in a garden centre for the past few months.' There was no need to tell him she was no longer required, and, remembering *why* she'd been forced to eke out her existence in such a manner, and in no mood now to prolong a conversation about her work, or lack of it, she got to her feet. 'Well,' she added abruptly, 'I'd better be going. I have a long drive ahead of me. It was nice to have met you, Mr Chevenay.' Reaching out, she picked up her portfolio.

'You no longer wish to do my gardens?' he asked blandly.

'Well, of course I want to do them! But you aren't going to let me, are you? So there's really no—'

'Aren't I?'

She just stared at him.

'You aren't the only one who grasps opportunities, Miss James.' Without waiting for her to comment, he got to his feet.

'You're going to let me *do* them?'

'Yes,' he agreed.

'Then why all the verbal games?' she demanded. He must have known how much this meant to her. 'If you knew when I came—'

'I didn't. I spoke to Mrs Davies,' he added briefly as he led her out and back through the front door.

'And that *cemented* your opinion, did it?' she asked waspishly. 'And she asked you to call her Davey.'

'What shall I call you?'

'Miss James,' she said promptly.

He gave a small grunt of laughter. It sounded reluctant.

Irritated, she demanded, '*Why* do you want me to landscape your gardens? You didn't yesterday.'

'Perhaps I feel the need to keep an eye on you.'

She snorted.

'Or perhaps I thought you needed the work.'

'You don't strike me as philanthropic,' she retorted dismissively.

'You don't want to do them?'

Of course she wanted to do them! But he would want references, wouldn't he? Any minute now he was going to ask for one. A man like Garde wouldn't take on just anyone. She had hoped—naively, she knew—that she could convince him of her capabilities so that he wouldn't ask. As she had hoped several times over the last few wretched months. And it had to be Nick behind it all, didn't it? But how could she prove it?

Sorrel was still staring at Garde, her gaze blank, when she suddenly realised that he was waiting for an answer.

'Yes, I want to do them,' she confirmed quietly, and then thought she'd better say something else to explain the long silence. 'I was just wondering why you hadn't used a local firm. There must be some.'

'There are. I even got a list of reputable landscapers. Countrywide,' he added softly. 'Your name wasn't on it.'

Well, it wouldn't be, would it? It had been taken off months ago. At Nick's instigation.

'You have references?'

No point in beating about the bush. 'No,' she said bluntly. 'I've never *needed* them,' she stated defiantly. Until recently.

He nodded. 'So what's the procedure?'

'Procedure?' she echoed. Astonished that references had been dismissed so lightly, she opened her mouth to query it, then hastily closed it again. Don't look a gift horse in the mouth, Sorrel.

'Yes,' he agreed with a slight edge of impatience. 'You make sketches? Dig holes? What?'

'Oh, sketches. You can then approve, or disapprove, let me have your own suggestions. Some people know exactly what they want. Others don't.'

'Then you may do some sketches for my approval.'

'Thank you. When would you like me to begin?'

'As soon as possible.'

Staring out over the front garden, she wondered why she didn't feel delighted. She should have done. Instead, she felt—wary. 'I'll need to know your likes and dislikes, whether you want trees, water features...'

'I don't know what I want. Be—inspirational, Miss James. You need to walk the course?' he asked, and then cursed.

Startled, she looked ahead and saw a young man leap out of a car by the broken gate. He had a camera slung round his neck.

'Who is he?'

'Very good, Miss James,' he mocked.

'What?' she asked in confusion.

'Your bewilderment looks almost genuine.'

'It *is* genuine! Why on earth would I—?'

'He's a reporter,' he interrupted. Come to check up that his protegé had gained access? he wondered. Possibly. Probably. Irritated with himself, and irritated with her, he added harshly, 'Just ignore him, and if he speaks to you don't answer.'

'But what does he want? Hey!' she exclaimed in shock as a flash went off, nearly blinding her. 'He just took my photograph!'

'Gilding the lily,' he muttered to himself. Ignoring the shouts for his attention, he directed her round the side of the house and out of sight.

'Gilding *what* lily?' she demanded in confusion.

'It's not important.'

Maybe not, but something was. 'Will he follow us?'

'No,' he denied grimly. 'Not if he values his equipment.'

'But what does he want?'

'To give me grief,' he said dismissively. 'You can use the utility room to store your tools or whatever,' he added as he halted to survey the tangled wreck of his walled rear garden. 'The gate at the end leads to a paddock—leased out to a local family for their horses. There's a lower field for vegetables, and this way…' He led the way across the broken terrace towards another wrought-iron gate that hung drunkenly by one hinge. 'There are half-demolished greenhouses, an old brick storeroom and a rubbish tip that is currently in the process of being cleared. But all that need concern you at the moment is the front.'

'And if you like what I do?' she prompted.

'Then you may do the back. I read something about parterres but, seeing as I wouldn't know a parterre if I fell over one, the point is moot.'

She doubted it. She suspected he knew very well what a parterre was, and anything else she might mention. He looked like a man who knew a great deal about a great many subjects.

'Come,' he ordered, still tersely, as he led the way back to the rear door. 'You'll need a room for sketching in.'

'I can do that outside or from the truck...' she began worriedly.

'Well, if you change your mind, you can use the old refectory,' he murmured as he led the way back inside. 'From when it was an abbey, of course.'

He threw open the first door on his left.

Stepping inside the long, empty room that echoed rather unnervingly, she stared round her. It was tiled in the same flags as the hall, but, unlike the hall, the room had yet to be restored. The arched leaded windows were uncurtained, the massive fireplace dusty. It looked as though it hadn't been used in a long time.

'I'll get a chair and table put in here for you to work at.'

'Thank you.'

'There's good light in here, and I imagine light is important for your sketching.'

'Yes,' she agreed as she walked over to the windows and stared out at the tangled rear garden.

He joined her. 'Once the cloisters, I believe, or cloistery—I'm never sure if it's singular or plural. There were other buildings originally—a chapel, sleeping areas, a dairy, a room where they made wine, stored their vegetables. There are still cellars...'

'Yes,' she agreed automatically as a sudden sparkle of light caught her eye. Sunshine reflecting off a piece of broken glass maybe, which reminded her of the reporter. 'Why would he take my picture?' she asked worriedly.

'The reporter? Who knows? Keeping up appearances?'

Bewildered, she began, 'What appear—?'

'It bothers you?'

'No-o,' she denied slowly, 'but he might think...'

'We have a romantic interest?' he asked derisively.

'There's no need to say it like that,' she scolded. '*Some* people find me attractive.'

'I dare say they do,' he agreed flatly.

She gave a small grin. He didn't sound as though he was one of them. 'Like your women with full figures, do you?' she asked tongue in cheek.

He looked at her, his eyes flat, unreadable. 'I like them silent.'

She gave a small snort of laughter and returned her attention to the garden.

'If the photograph is published,' he continued, 'is

there someone close to you who might be—offended?'

'No.'

'Good.'

Before she could ask him why it was good, he turned away and walked out, leaving her no choice but to follow. And, bizarrely, as though the room knew they had left, the door closed silently behind her. All by itself.

Staring at it, and then after the retreating Garde, she hurried to catch up with him. As though needing the reassurance of something solid, she trailed her hand across the uprights of the staircase and glanced up at the old maps decorating the rise to the landing. 'You collect them?'

He didn't answer. But then she hadn't expected him to. No doubt it was a hobby, or something. What other hobbies did he have? Apart from taking on unknown landscape artists and allowing dogs to visit? 'Do you really not believe I am who I say I am?'

He ignored her question, and she sighed. Subject closed? And why hadn't he pursued the subject of references? He wasn't a fool, so why take on someone—unknown? It didn't make sense.

'Don't worry about it,' he ordered with the same indifference as he turned at the study door. 'Just think of all that money you're going to charge me.'

'It isn't the money,' she denied quietly.

'Isn't it?' he asked as he opened the door and indicated for her to go inside. 'What else will you need?'

'Need?' she queried as she took two steps into the room and turned warily to face him.

'Yes.'

'Nothing until the sketches are approved.'

'Labourers?'

She shook her head. 'I usually do all the work myself.'

'Accommodation?'

'I'll book myself into the little hotel where I stayed last night.'

He nodded. 'An advance?'

Staring at him, feeling awkward—because she always hated this part, talking about money—for some silly reason her heart began to beat extraordinarily fast.

His regard was direct, penetrating, and those slate-grey eyes seemed to see into her soul. 'Why have you been working in a garden centre?'

Avoiding his gaze, she mumbled, 'Oh, well, you know, the winter and everything. People don't usually start thinking about their gardens until the spring.'

'It's now summer,' he pointed out drily.

'Yes, well…'

'Which presumably means your cash flow is—'

'Non-existent, right,' she interrupted staunchly. She still had a little in her savings account—what had been left from the sale of her house—but with rent and bills to pay for her tiny flat, it was being eaten away at an alarming rate. Her wages from the garden centre hadn't been very much.

'Then I'll arrange to pay your bill at the hotel, and

when you're ready for any outlay—turfs, plants—let me know.'

'Yes. Thank you.'

'Why so troubled?'

'I don't know.' And she didn't, not really, but Jen's words kept coming back to haunt her. *Was* she such a lousy judge of character? From wanting the job so badly, she now felt extremely troubled. Something just wasn't right about this. 'I didn't expect... I mean, I thought I would be leaving today. That I wouldn't see you again...' With a funny little shrug, she added, 'I'll need to go home, get my things...'

'When will you be back?'

She'd need a few days to get herself organised, do some washing and ironing... 'Monday?' she offered.

'Monday's fine.'

'I do know what I'm doing,' she insisted.

'I hope you do.' It sounded like a warning.

'But what I don't understand is *why*!' she exclaimed.

'No,' he said unhelpfully as he stared down into her wide eyes, 'I don't suppose you do.'

'And you aren't going to tell me?'

'Not yet. Don't worry about it, Miss James,' he mocked. 'I thought they were green.'

'Sorry?' she murmured, beginning to feel almost mesmerised.

'Your eyes. I thought they were green, but they aren't; they're blue with green flecks.'

'Yes.'

He gave a small, slow, smile that held not a trace of warmth, and then he kissed her.

CHAPTER THREE

A SLOW deliberate kiss that left her reeling.

'Why did you do that?' she gasped.

'Checking the height differential. What's the name of the garden centre?'

'Patterson's,' she answered almost blankly. Checking the *height* differential?

'In?'

'Fulham.'

'Then drive safely, and I'll see you on Monday.'

'Yes,' she whispered.

'And don't talk to the reporter.'

'No.'

He stepped to one side and she walked quickly out. Tugging open one half of the impressive front doors, she emerged into fitful sunshine. Why had he kissed her? Why? And why had he employed her?

'Miss? *Miss!*'

Ignoring the reporter at the bridge, she climbed into her truck and stared at the house. With her mind only half on what she was seeing, she gazed at the grey stone, the unruly creeper that straggled over the brickwork, and tried to imagine it as it had once been. Monks would have trodden these paths, hands tucked into their sleeves, tonsured heads bowed in prayer. There would have been a bell somewhere...

Glancing up, seeing nothing that resembled a bell tower, she sighed. Where had yesterday's feeling of fun gone? And *why* was there a reporter at the gate? Why *was* Garde famous?

Pull yourself together, Sorrel. Yes. But she really did need to know why he had kissed her, what he meant by 'height differential'. She wasn't going to work for him if he was going to be—heavy. Although he hadn't struck her as the sort of man who would press unwanted attentions on someone. She didn't want a serious relationship—not yet, anyway. It was far too soon after all the trouble with Nick and, although she had pretended to everyone that she was coping with it, she wasn't entirely sure she was.

Sorrel, she scolded herself, he doesn't even *like* you! So why had he kissed her? Because he had a girlfriend who was shorter than herself and he'd been curious to see what kissing someone taller would be like? Oh, don't be so stupid. It had been be- cause...well, because he was like Nick? No! He was nothing like Nick. Nothing at all! And Garde's grumpiness was obviously a front for—well, for something anyway. Feeling a bit muddled and un- easy, she fired the engine. If Jen hadn't said anything, she would have assumed that he was, well, flirting. No, she denied even more worriedly, he hadn't been flirting. So what *had* he been doing?

But she would be working again; that was the im- portant thing. Jen would probably give her grief, tell her she was being a fool, and maybe she was, but to be doing again what she loved doing...

Glancing at the front garden, her mind full of plans, she drove past the reporter without looking and began the long journey home.

'You're *what*?' Jen demanded.

'Going to work for him. And don't look at me like that; it's something I need to do.'

'I know, but...you don't know anything *about* him!'

'Look, I'm the big sister, right? And I won't need rescuing.'

Jen snorted.

'Baby sisters are supposed to *defer*!'

'Baby sisters who have more sense are supposed to look *after* their big sisters! And if you continue shoving things into your case like that there'll be nothing worth wearing when you get there! Here, give it to me!'

Abandoning the packing, Sorrel sat on the edge of the bed and let her sister do it. Younger, smaller, prettier, Jen had always been the efficient one. Sorrel was the dreamer. Jen's dark hair was thick and straight, her nose snub, her mouth wide. 'I'll be all right, you know,' Sorrel tried to reassure her.

'Then why didn't you tell me you were going to work for him when you first came home?' Jen demanded. 'If it was all above board...'

'Of course it's above board!'

'And what did he say about references?'

'Nothing.'

'Nothing?'

'No. He doesn't even *like* me.'

'Then why did he employ you? I think Giles ought to go down and check him out.'

'You dare,' Sorrel warned. 'I'm twenty-eight, Jen.'

'Yes, going on five. Little Marcus has more sense than you have.'

'Thanks!'

Turning, Jen gave a deep sigh. 'You will be careful, won't you?'

'Yes.'

'And get cash up front.'

'Yes.'

'And don't tell him *anything* about yourself. Don't go in the house...'

'Don't touch any money,' Sorrel muttered, more bitterly than she'd intended. 'Perhaps you ought to warn him.'

'Oh, Sorrel, don't,' Jen exclaimed. Sitting down beside her sister, she put her arms round her. 'I could *kill* Nick.'

'So could I.'

'Will you really be all right?' she asked eventually.

'Yes.'

'And you'll be staying in the same hotel you did before?'

'Yes. I booked a room before I left. I'll let you have the number as soon as I know it.'

'Borrow my mobile. I very rarely use it. Are you *sure* you're doing the right thing?'

'Yes,' she said positively. 'I need to work, Jen.'

'I know, but if—'

'Anything goes wrong, I'll come straight home,' Sorrel completed for her.

'Promise?'

'Promise. Don't you have *any* faith in me, Jen?'

'Well, of course I do! I just worry about you, that's all. You're so *trusting*!'

'Not any more,' Sorrel denied sadly. 'And Garde really isn't anything like Nick.'

'He's obviously wealthy if he can afford to buy an abbey.'

'But not like Nick,' Sorrel insisted. 'Did you manage to find out anything about why reporters might be haunting Garde's gate?'

'No,' Jen denied, and then she laughed. 'Although "haunting" is exactly the right word.'

Puzzled, Sorrel asked dubiously, 'Is it? Why?'

'Because the abbey is reputed to be haunted.'

Sorrel gave a scoffing laugh, and then paused as she remembered the door that had shut all by itself. No. She didn't believe in ghosts. 'They were probably there,' Sorrel decided, 'because Garde's some sort of entrepreneur. The wealthy are always newsworthy, aren't they?' Pausing again, she added slowly, 'Mrs Davies said he was hated.'

'Hated?'

'Mmm, by the reporters. Oh, well, I dare say I shall find out—and do take that worried look off your face, Jen. I shall be fine!'

Jen sighed. 'Are you sure he doesn't like you?'

'Yes!' Sorrel insisted. 'Why would he like me? I look like a stork!'

'You aren't in the least like a stork,' Jen protested, 'And I have never understood why you think yourself so unattractive. Men *like* you, Sorrel! Usually the wrong men, but...'

'Thank you,' Sorrel said drily.

'And if Nick hadn't wanted you...'

'None of this would have happened? You think I don't know that?'

'Because you didn't believe he could be attracted,' Jen stated. 'That's always been your trouble. You send out the wrong vibes.'

'I don't mean to. It just never occurs to me that men could find me desirable. I mean, look at me!'

'I am, and although I can't always see the attraction,' Jen teased, 'men do seem to think that—'

'I'm a good-time girl?'

'Well, yes.'

'And nothing could be further from the truth, could it? OK, I'll keep my lip buttoned.'

'And the amusement out of your eyes. Giles always says that you look as though you know things you shouldn't.'

'Like what?' Sorrel laughed.

'Er, the *Kama Sutra*?'

They both dissolved into giggles, but it was worrying all the same. Was that how Garde saw her? As a good-time girl? Was that why he'd kissed her? But a man like that probably had dozens of girlfriends. Sophisticated, elegant... 'From now on,' Sorrel promised, 'I shall present a sober and industrious face to the world.'

'But your face isn't made that way,' Jen protested. 'It always looks on the verge of laughter. Even with all you've been through—I'd have been suicidal. But you, you can be so—*philosophical*!'

'I didn't feel philosophical after it happened,' Sorrel confessed. 'I felt crushed.'

'I know that,' Jen whispered, with another hug, 'but other people thought you looked as though you didn't care.'

'And so they thought me guilty. But I couldn't give him the satisfaction of seeing how much he'd hurt me. I couldn't do that, Jen.'

'I know, love. I just wish there had been some way to prove that Nick is a liar. And to pursue his vendetta out of spite—well, I think he must be mentally unwell.'

'No, just vindictive. I should never have laughed at him. I didn't mean to; I was just so surprised when he declared his undying love. He was so theatrical about it all that I thought he was joking.'

'You made him look a fool.'

'Yes,' Sorrel agreed slowly. 'But how was I to know he'd told all his friends he was going to marry me? I mean, that was stupid!'

'Arrogant,' Jen corrected. 'He didn't expect to be turned down.'

No, because he'd expected her to be grateful, overwhelmed, honoured. Little Miss Nobody to marry a Right Honourable. She'd found out afterwards that

his family had been giving him hassle about marry-
ing, having sons. She'd also discovered that none of
the women in his own circle would have anything to
do with him. She didn't know why. Although, if he'd
behaved to them as he'd behaved to her... 'Water
under the bridge now,' she murmured. Hopefully.
Focusing back on her sister, she ordered firmly, 'But
for God's sake don't tell anyone I'm in Wiltshire!
Nick seems to know *everyone*!'

'Then let's hope he doesn't know Garde
Chevenay.'

'Yes. It has to have been Nick, doesn't it?' she
added quietly. 'Having me followed, telling the people I gave quotes to not to employ me.'

'Yes,' Jen agreed soberly. 'Not him personally—
someone he employed, I expect—but without
proof...'

'I know. Right,' Sorrel added briskly, 'I think
that's everything. I'll set off first thing in the morning. I won't wake you when I come to get my stuff
out of your garage.'

'No, don't,' Jen said humourously, 'and ring me
when you get there.'

'Yes, Mummy.'

Jen laughed and gave her sister a last hug before
leaving her to get some sleep.

The drive down was uneventful. Her arrival was uneventful. The rain had cleared away to leave a blue
sky. The reporter had gone, and so she halted in the
lane in front of the house and stared at the front

garden. She could see it in her mind's eye; how it could look, *would* look. A curved lawn sloping down to the stream; a sweeping gravel drive with a turning circle by the front doors. She hoped he didn't want the house enclosed by a security fence... Shrubs for easy maintenance; evergreens for winter interest; maybe a willow tree to overhang the water; and with the house tarted up, the windows clean and sparkling, the creeper trimmed, it would be beautiful.

Nothing fancy, she decided, just simple, clean lines to enhance. But first, she had to get it all cleared. She would start that first thing in the morning. For now, she would report in to Garde, drop off her equipment, have a good look at the lie of the land, and then drive to the inn and get her initial thoughts down on paper.

Putting the truck back in gear, she drove across the bridge and parked behind the blue van that had 'Kitchens' written on the side. Mrs Davies must have followed her advice. Anyone else, she thought in amusement, would have to wait months to get a kitchen installed. Garde obviously didn't.

Opening the utility room door, she began transferring her equipment.

'Do you need a hand?'

Startled, she turned quickly; she stared at Garde, stared into grey eyes that watched her without expression, and her heart gave a silly leap. A leap she hastily repressed.

'No,' she denied breathlessly, 'I can manage. I'll just unload my stuff, have a good look at the ground, do some sketches for your approval, and then make a proper start first thing in the morning.'

He nodded. 'Did you bring your portfolio back with you? I'd like to look at it again.'

'Oh, yes.' Hastily abandoning what she was doing, she reached into the truck, removed the photograph album and handed it to him. 'We can utilise anything you see in there that you like, but I would prefer to present you with my own sketches first. If that's all right,' she added quickly.

'Perfectly. Why so nervous, Miss James?'

'I'm not,' she denied hastily.

He gave a sceptical smile. 'Then I'll see you in the morning.'

'Yes.'

Rather surprised by his abrupt departure, she let all her breath out on a sigh. What did you expect, Sorrel? For him to be chummy? You don't *want* him to be like that. No. And she wouldn't go in the house; if the weather stayed fine, she could sketch outside, or if it was wet or cold, she could sit in the truck. Mrs Davies would maybe make her cups of tea, or she could bring a cold drink with her, and sandwiches. She told herself to just shut up and get on with it.

As soon as the truck was empty and everything was stored tidily in the utility room, she spent some time walking over the ground testing for unseen holes and obstacles that she would need to clear, but thankfully found nothing she hadn't been expecting. One of the old trees would need cutting down and uprooting and she might need some help with that. She would need to check out the local garden centres and hire a skip....

She continued her exploration, her mind busily counting out rough yardages for topsoil, turf, just in *case* he agreed with her ideas. On the other hand, he might want the whole lot paved, which would be a pity.

Finally finished, she drove to the hotel, booked in, and went up to her room to unpack. She rang Jen to assure her she was safely there, borrowed a local telephone directory and made some preliminary enquiries whilst eating the sandwiches she'd asked to be sent up. Then she sat on her bed to begin sketching out her ideas.

At eight o'clock she went down for her meal—and found Garde waiting for her.

'I thought I'd join you for dinner,' he informed her economically. No smile, no warmth: just a simple statement of fact.

'Right,' she agreed somewhat blankly. 'That's fine. Did you—?'

'Let the management know? Yes. I believe the dining room is this way.'

Bewildered, wrong-footed, she slowly followed him. 'Actually,' she said softly as he seated her at a table in the window, 'I was going to ask if you'd let Mrs Davies know.'

Handing her a menu, he shook his head. 'Mrs Davies isn't there.'

'You *dismissed* her?' she demanded in shock.

'No, and you shouldn't jump to conclusions. I gave her leave of absence while the kitchen's being done.'

'Oh.'

'Paid, of course. The steak pie is highly recommended.'

Feeling bewildered, and then perverse, she said shortly, 'I'll have the fish.' Snapping her menu shut, she stared at him. He stared back.

'You don't like her, do you?'

'I don't like indecision. Wine?'

'Who's paying?'

'I am.'

'Then, yes, please.'

His mouth twitched, just slightly, before he turned to summon the waiter who had been patiently waiting to attend the only two diners in the place. He was all of seventeen and looked bored to tears—which, seeing as Sorrel was the only guest in the small hotel at the moment, was only to be expected.

When Garde had ordered for them, he stared at her once more. 'What did you think of the kiss?' he asked slowly.

'What did I...?' she spluttered in astonishment. 'Well, really, what a thing to ask!'

He waited, watched, and she gave an alarmed snort. 'I didn't think anything of it!' she said. 'Why would I? It didn't mean anything.'

'You didn't enjoy it?'

'No,' she denied stonily.

'Why do you think I did it?'

'Well, I don't know, do I?' she exclaimed. 'Because you have a short girlfriend and you wanted to know what kissing someone taller would be like? Or, or—' she floundered.

'You didn't want it to mean anything?' he interrupted smoothly.

'No.'

His eyes smiled, almost. In anyone else she might have said it was disbelief, but with Garde, who could tell? Playing with her knife and fork, refusing to be dragged into a conversation she didn't want, she asked abruptly, 'Did you look at the portfolio again?'

'Yes. I don't want "pretty".'

'No,' she agreed. 'I thought... Hang on a minute.' Getting abruptly to her feet, she hurried out and up to her room. Grabbing her sketch pad off the dressing table, she ran back down. She returned slightly breathless, nearly knocking over the waiter, who was advancing with their meal. She hastily apologised, gave him a wide grin, and sat down, the sketchpad cradled on her lap.

'I'll show you my ideas when we've eaten.'

He nodded, thanked the waiter, and began on his soup.

There was obviously to be no small talk, no curiosity as the first course was finished and the second brought, and she felt a smile form in her eyes as she started on her fish. He was the most extraordinary man. Most people at least made an attempt at conversation, felt they needed to fill the silences, but obviously not Garde. Large and self-contained, with a dark remoteness about him that she found unbelievably attractive. Heaven knew why. A sunny person herself, she would have said, if asked, that she preferred people to be as she was. Open and light-hearted. Nick had been light-hearted. At first, anyway. And so perhaps her feelings about Garde were simply because he *was* so opposite to Nick. Recalling Jen's warnings, she was determined to be—cautious. She must suppress her natural instincts. Which Jen always insisted were hopelessly screwed anyway.

'Why the frown?'

Startled, she looked up to find him watching her, those slate-grey eyes so very penetrating, as though he would know all her thoughts.

'Mmm? Oh, nothing, just thinking.'

He nodded, as though accepting it, or not caring, she thought with an inward smile. He finished his meal, pushed the plate to one side, and sat cradling his wine glass.

Finishing her own meal, she did the same, and there they sat like Tweedle Dee and Tweedle Dum— only slimmer—just staring at each other. She felt her lips begin to twitch, tried to halt it, and then just had to give in to laughter.

His eyes reflected just a glimmer of amusement, and his strong face did relax slightly.

Their plates were removed and they were given the sweet menu. She chose chocolate pudding; Garde merely shook his head and returned the menus to the waiter.

'Why gardening?' he asked.

'I don't know,' she replied simply. 'I just love it. Making things grow. From the earliest age I can remember, it was all I wanted to do. I didn't make mud pies; I made flower beds. Patterns with stones, patterns with plants—I used to scream blue murder if I was forced to stay inside. So I don't know why, just something in my make-up. Mum was a teacher, Dad a plumber.'

'Was?'

'Yes,' she agreed with soft sadness. 'They both died years ago in an accident. And then there's Jen, my sister,' she added hurriedly because she really didn't want to talk about her parents. Not now. Not yet. It was still too painful. 'Before she married and started a family, she was an IT technician. My grandparents weren't gardeners, or not in a serious way. Why do you do what you do? Whatever that is?'

'Because I can. Coffee?'

'Please.'

Her sweet arrived and she ate it absently. She wanted to talk, tell him things, prolong the conversation, but she mustn't. Mustn't get close. Mustn't treat him as a best friend. Jen said that was what got her into trouble, being too friendly. Trusting people. But it was so hard not to, and surely, surely nothing would ever happen again like it had with Nick.

Staring down, she was almost surprised to find that she'd finished her pudding. She pushed her dish to one side and fought to keep her mind blank, to not *say* anything.

'I don't have a current girlfriend,' he stated. 'Short or otherwise.'

Flicking her eyes back to his, she found she didn't know what to say.

'So where does that leave the kiss now?'

Alarmed, she just stared at him, and he gave a slow smile, and, oh, what a difference a smile made.

'Don't do that,' she said without thinking and with a great deal of bemusement.

'Do what?'

'Smile. Secret weapons I can do without. Go back to being rude. You don't *like* me, Garde—Mr Chevenay,' she hastily remembered.

'Garde,' he corrected. And, damn him, he looked amused. 'Show me what you want.'

'What?' she gasped.

Eyes still holding hers, amusement deeper, he drawled drily, 'For the garden.'

'Oh.' Feeling a blush stain her cheeks, because for a moment she'd almost misunderstood, feeling stupid, she hastily picked up her sketchpad and handed it to him. 'Sorry.' Pulling herself together, she began, 'I thought a sweep of lawn down to the river, a willow...'

He gave her a look of mild derision, and she shut up.

Returning his eyes to the pad, he looked at all three drawings and then looked at them again, examined them more closely as his mind roved over the enigma that was Miss James.

She wasn't behaving at all as he'd expected.

Perhaps she was waiting until she'd entrenched herself before the questions started. And perhaps, a small voice warned, she was all that she said she was. No, he didn't believe that, but he was puzzled by her, by what seemed to be genuine *naivety*. What had she been doing since last summer? The letters in her portfolio only went up to last July. Had she done other work but not been praised for it? The garden centre had checked out, but every other answer she'd given had seemed evasive, and so he continued to probe for an explanation he could latch onto. He continued to try and keep her off balance. The trouble was, against his will he was beginning to like her. And that would be stupid.

'I'd like a Japanese Maple,' he announced without looking at her. Closing the pad, he gave it back to her. 'The first sketch. It's a lot of work for one person.'

'I can handle it.'

He nodded in acceptance and for that she was grateful. People never expected that she could do all the heavy lifting and hauling, but she could, and she wasn't stupid enough to take on something she was unable to do. She did know her limitations. Women accepted her prowess; men very rarely did. Most of the time they would insist on *helping*, when really she was better left on her own. She supposed women car mechanics, or plumbers, or whatever, had the same problem.

'How long will it take you?'

'Depending on the weather, probably about two weeks. I'll need to get a skip in.'

'So I imagined.'

'I was afraid you might want a six-foot boundary fence with spikes on top.'

'No. Anything else?'

She shook her head.

'Then I'll see you in the morning—with a rough estimate of cost,' he added. 'Goodnight, Miss James.' With a rather mocking smile that she didn't in the least understand, he left.

Staring after him, her face blank, all Sorrel could think was, Where does that leave the kiss now? She didn't think she was going to easily understand Garde Chevenay. Certainly she'd never met anyone like him before. And he probably *had* only employed her, as he had said, to keep an eye on her. Because he didn't trust her. Something you would do well to remember, Sorrel, she told herself.

At exactly eight o'clock the next morning, she parked behind the blue van. Collecting her camera, she unlatched her door and jumped down. Dressed in old jeans and a ragged sweater over an old T-shirt, she turned and came face to face with Garde. And found that she couldn't look away. He didn't move either, just continued to stare into her eyes, until finally, eventually, he gave a small nod towards her camera.

'For the portfolio?'

'What? Oh, yes.'

He nodded and turned away.

A little bit alarmed by her response to him, she watched him walk towards the rear and then suddenly remembered something she'd meant to ask him. 'Garde?' she called urgently, and he halted, turned.

'I forgot to ask you about the orchard. You want it left as it is?'

'Yes. Shout if you need anything.' Turning on his heel, he walked back towards the rear.

Garde had smiled, though. For *once* he'd smiled.

Will you *stop* it? she scolded herself. You're here to *work*! Determinedly slinging the camera strap round her neck, she began taking several shots from different angles of the front garden. Forcing away all thoughts of her employer, she replaced the camera in the truck, and, using Jen's mobile, she rang the number she'd written down to arrange for a skip to be delivered. She then walked into the utility room to collect her strimmer.

Two bottles of water and several hours later, her sweater had been removed and tossed on the front step. The long grass had been cut down and thrown in the skip and she'd made a start on removing the old turf. She didn't see Garde, just the man who was stripping out the old kitchen. He was young, slightly younger than herself at any rate, muscular, not unattractive, with fair hair hanging over his forehead. He would come out to his van, nod, comment—moan—about how hard his own work was, which at first amused her, then began to irritate her. Sorrel merely smiled in response. Settling in the sun, with her back to the house wall, she started the lunch that had been prepared for her by the hotel that morning. The builder joined her.

Suppressing a sigh, she forced herself to smile at him. 'How's it going?'

'Slow. They're a bugger, these old houses. Pipes are rotten, rendering's shot to pieces... Name's Sean, by the way.'

'Sorrel,' she commented briefly.

'Going to do it all yourself?'

'Yes.' Deliberately turning her gaze away, hoping he would take the hint, she stared at the old apple orchard that sat alongside the front garden and ran all along the side of the property. The trees looked pretty old and should have been pruned.

Finishing her sandwiches, she opened her flask.

'Got any of that to spare?' Sean asked hopefully.

'Mmm? Oh, yes, of course.' How fortunate there were two cups. Pouring him some tea, she hid her exasperation when he pulled a face.

'It's got sugar in.'

'Yes. Sorry.' There must be electricity in the kitchen, so surely he could have made his own tea? Hurriedly finishing her own, she got to her feet. 'Well,' she announced briskly, 'back to work.'

He stayed where he was. 'Going to take that old tree out?'

'Yes,' she agreed coolly.

'Won't be easy, that.'

'No.'

'Know him well? Garde?'

'No,' she said shortly. Packing up her lunchbox and flask, she put them in the truck and went back to work.

A few minutes later Sean disappeared, and she gave a sigh of relief. She didn't like interruptions when she was working. She smiled at herself when she realised she was being as grumpy as her boss!

She might not have smiled if she'd known that right at that moment Sean was reporting back to her employer.

'What did she ask you?'

'Nothing,' Sean replied. 'Not a solitary thing. I asked her if she knew you, and she said no. Just that. No embellishments, no curiosity, nothing.' And then he laughed. 'She didn't want to share her tea with me, either.'

With a small reciprocal smile, Garde thanked him. 'All right, I'll see you later.' Standing in his study, well back from her line of sight, he continued to watch her. She was a worker, he'd give her that. But, sadly, he couldn't give her his trust, which was a pity, because he was beginning to enjoy her company. Which was presumably why the reporter had employed her. Because she *was* good company. If she *was* employed by a reporter, which seemed more than likely. Certainly there hadn't been any reporters in evidence since she'd arrived.

Sorrel's hair was untidy, her face red with exertion and her arms scratched, Garde noticed as he watched her struggle to pull up a root. It gave way suddenly and she landed on her backside. Instead of cursing, or looking cross, or hurt, she laughed, and he turned swiftly away. He would do better to stay out of her way before he came to like her *too* much, this lady with the laughing eyes.

Used to the continuous roar of traffic in London, Sorrel found the silence of the countryside soothing, and for the first time in months she felt at peace. The abbey was surrounded mostly by farmland, although presumably there would be the odd tractor, ramblers maybe, to disturb the tranquillity. But for the moment there was nothing, just the rhythmic thud of the turf-cutter.

By five she had the lawn area cleared ready for levelling the next day. That shouldn't take too long, and then she could begin on the old trees, the flowerbeds, and maybe the stream.

After storing her equipment, she used the outside hose to wash her hands, and, with no sign of Garde still, she drove back to the hotel. Aching, and in dire need of a shower, she went thankfully up to her room.

Garde joined her for dinner again. He didn't say very much, merely commented on the fact that she'd caught the sun, asked if she wanted any wine, and then left as abruptly as he'd come.

That was the pattern for the rest of the week. Sometimes his car was parked at the house; sometimes it wasn't. And she knew no more about him now than she had at the beginning.

The plants she had chosen were delivered Friday morning. She set them out in their pots, rearranged them until she was satisfied, and then went to look for Garde to ask if he approved.

Remembering what had happened once before, with Nick, she didn't want to go into the house to look for him. She peered into his office window and, finding it empty, walked round to the kitchen. About to tap on the glass to attract the builder's attention, she stared, startled, at the mess inside. A pile of rubble filled one corner; the old sink was balanced on top. Pipes hung askew from walls that no longer had plaster and the air looked to be full of dust. Sean was sitting on an upturned crate, drinking something from a large mug. A tidy worker herself, she couldn't believe the mess he had created. Surely it would be easier to clear up as you went along?

With a little shake of her head, she tapped on the glass to attract his attention. He looked up, smiled, and came over to the open window.

'Sorry to disturb you…' she began.

'No problem. Want some tea? I managed to fit up an electric kettle.'

'No, thanks. I was looking for Mr Chevenay. Have you seen him?'

'End field, I think. That's where he was earlier, anyway.'

With a little nod and a half-smile, she walked through the walled garden and out at the far gate. She saw Garde in the distance. Shirt off, he was wielding a hoe. Well, maybe not *wielding*—more gently prodding with it.

Skirting the horses' field, she went to join him. Absorbed in what he was doing, and obviously listening to the cricket commentary on the small radio propped on the grass beside him, he didn't notice her at first, and she had time to stare, and be horrified by, the pink, lumpy scarring that covered his shoulderblades. Burns, she guessed, and not very old either. His neck, arms and waist were untouched.

Finally aware of her, he turned, his eyes expressionless. Expecting a look of horror on her face, he was surprised instead by sympathy. Concern. 'Not very pretty,' he commented.

'No,' she agreed inadequately. 'But at least you're being sensible and letting the air get to them. The pain must have been horrendous.'

'It was. What can I do for you?'

She gave a funny little movement, as though determinedly bringing herself back to the matter in hand, before saying quietly, 'I thought you might like to approve the arrangement of plants before I put them in.'

He nodded, stuck his hoe in the ground, collected his shirt from a nearby bush and put it on. He'd barely seen her all week; in fact he'd deliberately avoided her, apart from the meals at the hotel, and he'd been rather surprised that she hadn't sought him out, whatever the pretext. He'd watched her, and waited, and nothing had happened. She hadn't been in the house, nor into his study. There had been no snooping, no questioning Sean. He'd also expected her to know about his back, and she didn't seem to. Either she was a very good actress, or...

Keeping his thoughts to himself, he accompanied her round to the front. Still no reporter. 'Very nice,' he approved quietly as he obediently stared at the plants, then deliberately walked away.

Had he been embarrassed that she'd seen his back? she wondered as she began to slowly put the plants in and then give them a good water. No, she decided, she doubted Garde would be embarrassed. She wondered how it had happened. The article about him hadn't mentioned an accident, but then the magazine had been six months old. Was that why so little work had been done on the house? Because he'd been in hospital or something?

None of your business, Sorrel. No.

With a small sigh, she put all her things away, gave a last glance at the arrangement of plants, then nodded in satisfaction and drove back to the hotel.

That night, Garde didn't join her for dinner. And she missed him. As uncommunicative as he was, she missed him. It's what you wanted, she reminded herself. Yes. Keeping a distance from each other was best. So why didn't it feel like it?

She didn't sleep very well for thinking about Garde, about his back, about the way he was, and she woke early, feeling unrested. A few more days and the front would be finished. Would he then want her to start on the back? She had no idea. She didn't know if he liked what she'd done so far; there had been no praise, no commendation, almost as though he didn't care what it looked like. She gave a small smile. So long as it wasn't 'pretty', he'd said.

Well, she didn't need praise; she was *professional, businesslike,* she assured herself. Wrong. She *wasn't* businesslike. She hated presenting people with her invoice, hated having to discuss money, *justify* it—because she always made friends out of the people she worked for, and it was hard to ask them for money. Except for Garde, of course, who wasn't a friend.

Still feeling unsettled, she dressed in clean old jeans and a T-shirt and drove out to the abbey. She halted in the lane in order to get an overall view of how everything was coming along and get her perspectives right. Switching off the ignition, she turned to look—and then just stared in disbelief. In shock.

All the plants she had so painstakingly put in the day before had been uprooted.

CHAPTER FOUR

STUNNED with unimaginable horror, almost unable to take it in, she opened her door, climbed out, stepped over the stream, and wanted to weep. Bushes, shrubs had just been yanked up and thrown onto the area marked out for lawn.

Raising her eyes, she stared at Garde as he stood surveying the mess. 'What did you *do?*' she cried.

'Not me,' he stated flatly. 'You think I would do this?'

'Then who? Why?' she began disjointedly.

'I don't know. Will they recover if we put them back?'

'Maybe. Some,' she agreed dully.

'Then let's do it,' he suggested quietly.

Glancing at him, seeing no expression on his face at all, she returned her gaze to the poor plants. 'But who would *do* such a thing? I mean, we can't blame it on the ghost, can we?'

'Ghost?'

'The abbey is supposed to be haunted, isn't it?'

'Oh, so they say.'

'You didn't see anything? Hear anything?'

'No.'

'No,' she agreed blindly. And it wouldn't be Garde, would it? No, don't be ridiculous, Sorrel. 'A neighbour? The reporter?' she offered. 'Only Mrs Davies said—'

'That I was hated?'

'Yes,' she agreed miserably.

'It's possible.' But not likely, he thought. He'd already run through every possibility and come up with nothing. This had been done out of spite. And he didn't think he could bear the expression on her face. With a bitter smile, he deliberately squashed any feelings he might have. He didn't know her, certainly didn't know if he could trust her, didn't even know if she'd done this *herself*, although it didn't seem very likely. He was continually waiting for the cracks to show, and he was finding it very frustrating that they hadn't. Yet. 'Don't cry,' he said brusquely as he caught sight of the tears trembling on her lashes.

'I'm *not*!' she denied fiercely as she scrubbed the tears away 'But how could someone *do* this? How *could* they?'

'I don't know.'

There was a toot from the lane and they both turned to look. Her truck was blocking the path and Sean's van couldn't get past.

'I'll move it,' Garde said shortly. Mouth tight, he strode across and drove the truck across the bridge and parked in front of the garage.

'Bloody hell,' Sean exclaimed as he stepped out of his van. 'Who did that?'

'I don't know.'

'Is she all right?'

'What do you think?' he asked tersely. Walking back to stand beside Sorrel, he stared at her distressed face. 'Giving in to it won't help,' he stated. 'Get angry, mad, but don't give in.'

She turned anguished eyes up to his, and then firmed her mouth. 'Is that what you do? Get mad?'

He gave a cynical smile that she didn't understand. 'Yes.'

'Very well. I won't give in.'

He nodded, picked up two of the plants himself and moved them onto the flowerbed.

'Not there,' she said as she elbowed him to one side and moved them. She didn't understand his attitude; he seemed almost uncaring of what had happened. And that hurt her almost as much as the damage to the plants. 'Has anything else happened?'

'No.'

'Your vegetable patch?'

'No. Tell me where you want them.'

Fetching her spade, she directed him, and then they put everything back. It took two hours, but they didn't look the same. Not as nice, and her feeling for them had gone. They watered them in and then just stood and stared at them.

'We can replace any that die,' he said quietly.

'It's not the point, though, is it? Should we report it to the police?'

'I already did. Not that they can do anything.'

'You don't seem very—bothered.'

'Don't I? That's probably because you don't know

me very well,' he said dismissively. 'Is there anything else I can help you with?'

She shook her head. 'The turfs should be here soon. They said midday. I'll finish levelling off the lawn area.'

He nodded. 'I have to go out for a while. You'll be all right?'

'Yes.'

'I've asked the builder to keep an eye out.'

She gave a small, sad smile. She didn't think the builder would be much use in an emergency. Not on what she'd seen of him so far, anyway.

When Garde had gone, feeling dispirited, she went to get her rake and level. Who? she kept wondering. Why? If it had happened in London she would immediately have suspected Nick, but Nick didn't know where she was. Or did he? No, she assured herself, that was paranoia. And even if he had, he would have written to Garde, or come to see him, as he had other clients before. Well, that she *assumed* was what had happened before. She didn't actually have any proof that it was Nick who'd put off prospective customers. But *someone* was responsible—and that someone might come back.

She thought about it continually, worrying all around it, and as she did so she began to get angry. Not only about the garden, but about Garde too. Blow hot, blow cold. Nice one minute, terse the next. The first job she'd had in *months* and now this. Perhaps it wasn't directed at Garde, but at herself. Perhaps she'd trodden on somebody's toes. She'd

been a bit dismissive of the plants in the first garden
centre she'd looked in. And the owner had been a
bit angry at her scathing comments, hadn't he?

She was too churned up to even eat her lunch. She
laid the turfs, tramped them down, watered them, and
then stood at the end of the garden to survey her
handiwork. The new Japanese Maple that stood in
the waist of the elongated S-shape of the lawn looked
a bit sad; she might need to replace that. The others—well, tomorrow would show more. Either they'd
survive or they wouldn't. But if they came back—
whoever 'they' were—then she would be waiting,
she decided. If she had to sit up all night, she would
do so.

With Garde still not back, she packed up her tools
and locked them away, then drove back to the hotel.
She barely picked at her meal. Glad that for once
Garde didn't join her, she absently chased her food
around her plate. She wanted to *do* something. Why
shouldn't she wait up to see if the vandals came
again? she suddenly thought. Nothing was likely to
happen until dark, was it? She had plenty of time to
get ready. And if they did come back…

Pushing her uneaten meal aside, not waiting for
coffee, she hurried up to her room. Changing into
dark trousers and a dark sweatshirt, she felt a bit
theatrical and silly. She grabbed her small torch, a
pad and a pen, and rang down to ask if a flask could
be prepared for her. Explaining that she had to go
out, and not to worry if she was late back, she drove
out towards the abbey.

The sky was just beginning to darken as she carefully manoeuvred the truck into a stand of trees opposite the orchard. Checking that she was hidden from view, she ran furtively along the lane to see if Garde was back. There were no lights showing in the house; neither was his car out front. Wouldn't it be amusing if he was keeping watch from a darkened room while she was hiding in the bushes? Maybe she should have told him what she was intending to do. Although the way he'd been behaving this week, she didn't feel like telling him anything.

She hurried back to the car and settled down to wait.

And wait.

And wait.

Was Garde there? she wondered. It seemed a bit odd to go off and leave the house unattended after what had happened. Perhaps he didn't care. Certainly he hadn't seemed very bothered earlier. Maybe he'd been expecting it? Or something like it? He certainly was a strange man, hard to get to know, and yet she found herself forever thinking about him. Like wondering how he'd got those scars on his back. Where had he got them? And did that account for his bad temper—because they were still painful?

She watched the moon sail into view. She listened to the furtive sounds in the undergrowth, the eerie hoot of an owl, and shivered. There were no street lamps to illuminate anything, just the moon that created worrying shadows. Feeling like a fool, nervous, she jumped as a branch cracked somewhere.

Stop it, she scolded herself, there's nothing out there; but she picked up her torch and switched it on for comfort. She checked her watch for the umpteenth time, yawned, shifted her position. There was no danger of her falling asleep—she was much too jumpy—and no one was coming, were they? It had been a one-off. Probably vandals, or a drunk. Someone had seen her put the plants in and thought it would be amusing to pull them out.

Ten past two. Go back to the hotel, Sorrel, she told herself. Get some sleep. Five more minutes, she decided. She picked up her flask, unscrewed the lid, and then froze. Tilting her head, she listened hard. Was that a car?

Screwing the top back on the flask, trying to ignore the nervous flutter of her heart, she put it carefully on the floor. She rested her arms on the steering wheel, peering ahead through the trees.

It was definitely the sound of an engine, but there were no lights. And it was definitely a car, she finally saw. It was creeping slowly along the lane—and if that wasn't furtive, she didn't know what was. It halted a little way down from her and the engine was switched off.

She held her breath, waiting as she watched a figure step out and push the car door to, not shutting it properly. A man carrying something climbed over the low fence that surrounded the orchard and disappeared into the trees.

She unlatched her own door, picked up the pad, pen and torch from the passenger seat, and quietly

followed. Careful to make no noise, she shielded her
torch with her trembling hand. She jotted down the
car's make and registration number and then crept
after him. She had no idea what she was intending
to do—just watch, she supposed vaguely, so that she
could maybe identify him later. She certainly wasn't
intending to confront him, whoever he was. She
wasn't *that* much of a fool. But when she saw him
walk to the middle of her newly laid lawn and un-
screw the cap of the can he was carrying, all rational
thought fled.

With an ear-piercing screech, she launched herself
over the small fence that divided the orchard from
the garden and, before he could do more than swing
round in surprise, rugby-tackled him to the ground.

There was a shout from the house. A light that
was brighter than any searchlight had a right to be
shone over the lawn and she squinted, refusing to let
go of the man she was struggling with. The undig-
nified gripping, grasping struggle that was underway
was only going to have one ending. He was stronger
than her, probably fitter than her, and she didn't
know if it was herself grunting or him as he fought
to get free. Dazed, but damned if she was going to
let him get away with it, she grabbed his foot as he
began to rise, and as he wrenched it free it caught
her a stunning blow in the ribs.

With a grunt of pain, she curled herself into a ball,
and felt rather than saw her attacker run away.
Moments later there was the sound of a car engine

being urgently revved and the squeal of tyres as he took off too fast. She hoped he crashed.

'What in *God's* name do you think you were doing?' Garde demanded savagely as he knelt beside her.

Furious, feeling victimised, she shouted raggedly, 'Well, *you* weren't doing anything!'

'I was doing a great many things. Where are you hurt?'

'Ribs, head—oh, I don't know,' she exclaimed irritably. 'And now he's getting away.' Remembering what he'd been doing, she snapped upright. 'He had a can...'

'I *know* he had a can, and if you hadn't interfered—'

'*Me*, interfere?' she exclaimed. 'Am I psychic? You might have *told* me what you were going to do.'

'As might *you*,' he said tensely. 'Can you get up?'

'No,' she muttered, 'And if that stuff's leaking...'

He murmured something as he reached out to right the can, and finally located the lid and screwed it tightly on before helping Sorrel to her feet.

Arms round her sore ribs, she allowed him to help her into the house. 'I had a pad of paper,' she began grumpily. 'I must have dropped it.'

'I'll find it later,' he said impatiently as he helped her into the study and sat her in his swivel chair behind the desk. 'Let me have a look.'

'No,' she said as she hunched over.

'Are they broken?'

'I don't know.'

'Then let me see.'

With a cautious sigh, she slowly straightened up.

'Breathe normally,' he ordered.

'I can't,' she said childishly. 'It hurts.'

'Then perhaps that will teach you not to tackle intruders.' Pushing her gently back, he lifted her sweater and softly touched his fingers to her ribs.

'Ouch.'

'I don't think they're broken.'

'Good.' Leaning her elbow on the edge of the desk, she closed her eyes, put her head against her open palm, and then rapidly lifted it with a cry of pain. There was blood on her fingers.

'He *cut* me!'

He sighed.

She could feel him watching her and she slowly raised her head. She stared at him, at a face so harshly carved she could see no sympathy there, just a sort of blank impatience. She sighed again, leaned back and closed her eyes. 'You weren't in bed,' she stated.

'No,' he agreed as he gently examined the cut that was beginning to swell. His fingers tickled as he carefully pushed her hair to one side. It felt intimate.

Slapping his hand away, because his touch, his nearness, was making her feel breathless, which irritated her even more, she asked raggedly, 'Did you recognise him?'

He shook his head.

'I got his car number. It's on my pad. The police could probably trace him. Have you rung them?'

'No.'

Snapping open her eyes, she demanded, 'Why not?'

'Because I haven't had time! Do you want to go to the hospital?'

'No.'

'The cut's not deep; it doesn't need stitching. I'll get you a plaster, some aspirins and a cup of tea. After I've rung the police,' he added pointedly. Picking up the phone, he punched out the number of the local police station, tersely explained what had happened, and walked out.

After slamming open the kitchen door with a violence it didn't deserve, he snapped on the light, stared at the mess within, then gave a bitter smile. For one awful, stupid, impulsive moment he'd wanted to cradle her against him, make her better. Yeah, right, he derided himself as he put the kettle on to boil. He should never have employed her. He should have let her go, let her take whatever story she wanted. What the hell did it matter? But she *was* a gardener. He had to give her that. She was definitely someone who knew about gardens. But what else was she? Someone who amused him, he thought wearily, and it had been a long, long time since he'd felt amused. She was tall and gangly, pushy, irritating. Gutsy, he admitted. And now this. She could have been killed. They would pay for that, he decided grimly. Whoever they were.

He *wanted* to trust her, but he couldn't afford to—couldn't afford to trust anyone he didn't know. He had learned that to his cost a long time ago. And he hated it, being suspicious of every passing stranger. And he was attracted to her, he admitted for the first time. Not just liking, or amused, but attracted. Heaven knew why, he thought wearily. She wasn't his type at all.

With an irritable gesture he made the tea and carried it back to the study. Edging open the door, he halted and stared at her. She was leaning back in his chair, her eyes closed, the bottom of her sweatshirt tucked up beneath her chin, and she was gingerly feeling her ribs. Her hair was a tangled mess, her face dirty, as were her hands, and he felt an absurd rush of—something—for this very strange girl. She was like no one he had ever met. A refreshing change, he would have said—if he could have trusted her.

'Tea,' he announced abruptly, and she opened her eyes.

Turning her head, she gave a small grimace and pulled her sweater back down. She looked wary, he thought, and wondered why.

He handed her the tea, walked round the desk and opened the top drawer. Taking out a box of plasters and some wipes, he cleaned the wound with maximum efficiency, then peeled off a dressing and stuck it carefully over the cut on her temple. He replaced the packet, removed a bottle of painkillers, shook out two and handed them to her.

'Thanks. I didn't want him to ruin the lawn,' she

added by way of lame explanation. She found it extraordinarily difficult to look Garde in the eye.

'No,' he agreed.

'All I really meant to do was get his car number and a rough description. I didn't know you were— prepared. I thought you'd be asleep. Or still out. Your car wasn't there.' She sounded accusing.

'It's in the garage.'

'Oh.' Swallowing the painkillers with another little grimace, she took a hasty sip of tea. It tasted strong enough to strip paint. Putting the mug back down, hands clasped round it, she gave him an almost furtive glance. Stubble was beginning to darken his chin and he looked dangerous again, as he had the first time she'd seen him. Large and grim. Powerful. 'I should have let you tackle him, shouldn't I?' she stated quietly. Annoyed with herself, because for some stupid reason she felt shy and awkward, she added even more foolishly, 'Although you might have hurt your back.' Unable to stifle her yawn, she leaned back and stared at the bookshelf. 'I thought you weren't interested in my plants.'

'Then you thought wrong, didn't you? I'll go and see if I can find your pad.'

Grateful for the reprieve, she nodded and watched him depart. He was angry. About her, or the vandal, or both. And he'd been prepared. Swivelling the chair round, she stared out of the window at a scene as bright as day. Light flooded everything. She should have left it to him. Although how was she supposed to have known that he was going to do something when he hadn't *said*? But then, she hadn't said anything either. A severe lack of communication. And just what *was* it about him that made her so unsettled? She'd been fighting it for days—successfully, she'd thought. And now... You're tired, she told herself impatiently, that's all. Tired and hurt and feeling stupid.

She heard the front door close, followed by his footsteps on the stairs. Listening carefully, she could hear soft thuds from above her, and then the spotlight went out and all she could see was her own reflection in the glass. Seconds later she heard his footsteps descending, and felt nervous again. How stupid. Why on earth would she be nervous of him? Because it was late? Dark? The fact that they were alone in his house? And what did she know of him, after all? Nothing.

Swivelling the chair, she watched the door, saw it open. Apart from her pad, which he tossed towards her, he was carrying a small, square black box which he placed on the desk.

'Camera,' he stated shortly.

She hadn't thought of that. She *should* have done. Not that her camera had a flash. Not that the shops had been open to buy one. At least, not by the time she'd decided what she was going to do. 'I didn't think things through very well, did I?' she asked disgustedly.

'No. How do you feel?'

'OK. A bit dizzy, achy. I can hear a car.'

'The police, I expect.'

Risking a glance, she asked eventually, 'Why didn't you tell me you were setting a trap?'

'You didn't ask.'

No, she hadn't asked.

'Do them often, do you?' he asked drily.

'What?'

'Stake-outs.'

'Oh,' she murmured on a tired sigh. 'No.'

'Where did you leave your truck?'

'In some trees the other side of the orchard.' With a small, self-conscious grimace, she added, 'Miss Marple, I'm not.'

'No. It was a good rugby tackle, though.'

'Yeah, for all the good it did me. He wasn't very old,' she added after a few moments' silence. 'In his late teens, I'd guess.' There was the crunch of tyres on gravel and she turned to glance from the window once more. She could just make out the police car.

They didn't stay long; they merely took statements from them both, took the camera and the note she'd made of the car and the registration number and left, promising to keep in touch. They also told Sorrel how stupid she'd been to tackle the man.

Sorrel watched Garde return from seeing the policemen off and go over to the window to stare out into the night. Able to watch him now that he wasn't watching her, she asked without thinking, 'How did you hurt your back?'

Ah. Finally, the questions he'd been expecting. Disappointed, he answered briefly, 'Helicopter crash.'

'Was anyone else hurt?'

'No.'

'You should oil it.'

'The helicopter?'

'No, silly, your back.'

'Can't reach,' he stated dismissively.

'And you don't know anyone who would do it for you?' she asked in disbelief.

'No one I would want to ask.'

'Oh.'

Turning, he asked quietly, 'Offering, are you, Sorrel?'

She shook her head, then wished she hadn't as a wave of dizziness assailed her. 'I should go back to the hotel.'

'And possibly meet up with your attacker, who might now bear a grudge?' he asked derisively. 'I don't think so. I'll make you up a bed here.'

'No.'

'Yes. Don't go to sleep,' he ordered.

She sighed. 'No.'

'Come on, you can help.'

Letting all her breath out, she levered herself to her feet.

'Take tomorrow off.'

'I'll see how I feel.'

He led the way upstairs and along the landing to a door at the end. Pushing it open, he herded her inside.

There was an unmade-up bed. And that was all.

He walked out and returned moments later carrying some sheets, pillowcases and a couple of blankets, which he dumped on the bed. 'Bathroom's next door. Do you want something to sleep in?'

She started to shake her head, then remembered not to. 'No,' she said quietly.

'Then I'll see you in the morning. Don't go wandering in the night.'

'Or the ghost might get me?' she asked sleepily.

'Something like that.'

And then she remembered, suddenly, that she shouldn't be in his house at *all*, never mind the ghost. Jen had said so. 'Garde...' she began urgently, and he halted, turned. 'I can't stay here.'

'Don't be ridiculous,' he said dismissively as he turned away again.

'But I can't!' She hurried towards him and touched his back; he flinched. 'Sorry,' she whispered, and snatched her hand away.

Turning again, he stared at her. He was too close, too masculine, too large, and she felt—strange.

There was an expression of almost distaste on his face as he asked flatly, 'What is it you want?'

'Want?' she echoed as her mind registered the warmth of him, the faint scent of aftershave or soap, or something. There was a small scar at the edge of his left eyebrow, a dirty mark on his chin, and his mouth was...

'Sorrel!' he ordered impatiently. 'What is it you *want*? To know about the crash? My business ventures? Ask me tomorrow, when I'm not so tired and perhaps more in the mood for games.'

'It's not a game,' she whispered with a frown. 'I want you to…'

'Kiss you?' he snapped.

She blinked, frowned again. 'No.'

'No?' he derided. 'Then what? A little light dalliance? A seduction?'

'No,' she denied dizzily. 'I want you to wait.' Oh, this was stupid. Feeling muddled and tired, and feeling not very well at all—she was in shock, she supposed—she slumped against the doorframe, trying to ignore the effect his nearness was having on her. 'Is there any money in the house?'

'Money?'

'Yes.'

'You need some?' he asked flatly.

'No.'

'Then go to bed.'

She watched him walk the length of the landing and go into a room at the other end. She hadn't explained that very well, had she? And now he would think… Without even *considering* what she was doing, she hurried after him and pushed open his door. 'Garde…'

He swung round, his face set. 'Go *away*!' he thundered.

'But I didn't explain…'

Advancing, he grasped her shoulders and turned her. 'I don't want you to explain. I want you to go to your room and go to sleep! Alone.'

'I always sleep alone,' she answered hazily. Why

was the room spinning? Clutching the doorframe, she
felt her knees begin to go. Puzzled, rather than
alarmed, she turned her head to look at him, and
passed out.

CHAPTER FIVE

'OH, FOR God's sake,' he began. Disappointed in her, infuriated, thinking it was a ploy, he yanked her upright. She was like a boneless doll. Realising, belatedly, that she *wasn't* faking, he became suddenly frightened. He hoisted her into his arms and laid her on his bed. Her eyelids fluttered and then opened, and he doubted anyone, even the best actress in the world, could have conjured up such a look of bewilderment.

'Don't ask where you are,' he ordered with soft irony, and forced himself to distance his mind, his body.

She blinked, continued to stare at him.

'You passed out.'

She gave a funny little shudder, swallowed, then licked her lips. 'I've never fainted in my life,' she whispered.

'You have now. How do you feel?'

'A bit—strange. Sorry.'

'My fault. I should have taken you to the hospital.'

She shook her head, and winced. 'I really must stop doing that.' Lifting a shaky hand, she touched it to her temple. The swelling was bigger. Like an egg. 'I'll be all right now.' She moved as though to get up, but he gently pushed her down again.

'Lie still.'

'The shock, I expect.' Or the fact that she hadn't eaten much that day.

'Yes,' he agreed. 'Who are you, Sorrel?' Now was probably not the right time to ask, but he really did need to know.

'Who?' she asked in puzzlement.

'Yes. Why did you really come here?'

'To do your garden.' Searching his face, a little frown in her eyes, she exclaimed, 'Why else would I come but to do your garden?'

'To find out about me.'

'Find out what?'

He gave a small sigh. 'That's what I want to know.'

Moving her head into a more comfortable position, she continued to stare at him. 'You have a dirty mark on your chin.'

'Do I?'

'Yes. You asked me if I wanted you to kiss me. Why?'

'Because I thought it was the big seduction scene.'

'I'm not built for seduction.'

'Aren't you?' he asked gently.

'No. Is it my eyes?'

'Eyes?'

'Yes, only my sister said—' Breaking off, she gave another little frown. Why on earth were they having this absurd conversation?

'Your sister said?' he prompted.

'That my eyes make people think I know more

than I do. And I don't. That's really annoying me,' she murmured as she lifted a hand to wipe the mud from his chin.

With a rather dry smile, he captured her wrist and showed her the state of her hand. It was far, far muddier than his chin.

She gave a gentle, rather bewildered smile.

'Why did you ask about money?'

'Because...' Searching his face, deciding it might be best to be honest, she said quietly, 'Because I was once accused of taking some.'

'From someone you worked for?'

'Yes. I couldn't prove I didn't, and Jen said—'

'Your sister?'

'Yes. She said not to go in your house. But I told her you weren't like him. You don't know him, do you? Only I thought for a minute that it might have been him taking the plants, but of course it wasn't. He doesn't know where I am.' Feeling sleepy, shivery, she snuggled into the bedcover and closed her eyes.

Staring down at her, feeling really rather baffled, he gently lifted the quilted cover that hung to the floor and draped it over her, then wondered if he should allow her to sleep. Weren't you supposed to keep people awake if they had head injuries? With a deep sigh, he wondered what it was about him that brought so many complications into his life. He stared longingly at the empty side of the bed. And she really shouldn't be left alone, should she? Oh, to hell with it. If she wanted to make capital out of it she would. But wouldn't it be nice if she were exactly who she said she was? Against his will, she was beginning to fill his thoughts to the exclusion of all else. So who was the fool now?

He kicked off his shoes, went to collect another blanket to cover himself, then lay down beside her. Sleep had been in rather short supply of late—something courted, but very rarely achieved since the accident. But when he'd left her at her door he had thought himself tired. Tired enough to fall dreamlessly asleep, for once.

With a grim smile, aware of the weight of her against his back, he determinedly closed his eyes, listened to her quiet breathing, the odd noises the old house made as it settled, until finally he drifted off to sleep.

Brightness against her lids woke her from a jumbled dream of ghostly monks carrying plants. She could still almost hear their deep, regular breathing as... Snapping open her eyes, she lay very, very still and stared at the bright square of sunlight on the wall opposite her. She *could* hear deep, regular breathing. There was also a heavy, warm weight at her back.

She'd fainted, she remembered. Absurd as it seemed, she'd actually fainted, and Garde had laid her on his bed, where she presumably still was, and Garde was—sleeping with her?

Afraid to move in case she woke him, she eased her left arm out from under the covers and glanced at her watch. Eight o'clock. And it had been, what?

After four when they'd come upstairs? Must have
been. And four hours' sleep wasn't enough for anyone. So why had she woken? She could hear a bird
singing somewhere outside, and she was still fully
clothed, she discovered to her relief. Was *he*?

He stirred, and she froze again, her eyes wide. Oh,
for goodness' sake, she scolded herself, he's only
asleep! Be insouciant! Roll onto your back, yawn,
get up! Don't just lie here like a ninny. Turning carefully, restricted by the cover that cocooned her, she
stared at the back of his head. Saw his shirt collar
just above the yellow blanket he had over him. His
hair was thick and dark, with a slight curl, tousled,
begging for her fingers to untangle it. No, Sorrel, she
told herself firmly. It was tempting, though. Very
tempting. As were the broad shoulders. Wrapped as
she was in the quilt, she couldn't actually feel the
rest of him against her, only the heavy weight holding the cover down, but it still felt—intimate.

She wanted to blow on the back of his neck, put
her arms round him, be held. It had been a long time
since she'd been held. And she liked him; she was
curious about him. Folly. Absolute folly. But it
would be nice just to...

'I gather you're awake,' he said quietly, and she
gave a nervous start.

'Yes,' she blurted, and he heaved himself over in
the wide bed. Stared at her.

'How do you feel?'

'Fine,' she said quickly.

'Sure?'

'Yes. Thank you.'

'For what?' he asked lazily.

She stared back at him, feeling disorientated. 'I don't know.'

He smiled, and she felt—hot.

'It's been a long time since I woke up with a woman beside me,' he murmured, almost provocatively.

'Is it?' she asked worriedly.

'Yes. Are you really who you say you are?'

'Yes.'

He searched her eyes, her face, as though he would find the truth there, and finally gave a small nod. He was so very tired of pretending to be something he wasn't. If she wasn't who she said she was, well, he would have to learn to live with it, wouldn't he? 'Good morning.'

She gave him an inane smile, which seemed to amuse him. Nervous, inarticulate, she untangled her arm and shoved her unruly hair off her face. Encountering the bump, she gingerly felt it.

'How is it?'

'Not too bad.'

'Good. You frightened me to death.'

'I doubt it,' she derided huskily, 'and don't smile.'

'Ah, no, I forgot. Something about a secret weapon, wasn't it?'

'Yes. I can't get up.'

'Can't you?'

'No. You seem to be lying on some of the cover.'

Moving his right arm, he crooked it, lifted his head

to rest on his palm and continued to survey her. 'You look nervous,' he observed softly.

'I'm not in the least nervous,' she lied loftily.

'Who was the man who accused you of stealing?'

Hastily lowering her eyes, she stared at his chest. 'I told you, someone I worked for.'

'*Why* did he accuse you?'

She shrugged.

'Sorrel...' he warned softly.

'He wanted to marry me,' she blurted.

'And you didn't want to be married?'

'No.'

'And so he accused you of *stealing*?' he asked in disbelief.

'Yes. He was my boss, so when some money went missing, he took it as his opportunity to discredit me. He knew I wasn't the thief; he was being vindictive.' She glanced at Garde, and saw the rather sceptical expression on his face. She sighed. It did sound pretty unbelievable, but that was what had happened. 'I'd like to get up now,' she said firmly.

'No dalliance?'

'No.'

He searched her face for what felt, to her, like for ever, then rolled to one side, untucked the quilt that was holding her captive and then resumed his former position.

With her eyes wide, feeling wary, relieved—disappointed?—she continued to stare back at him.

'You changed your mind?' he asked softly when she didn't move.

'No! No,' she denied more mildly. Shoving the yellow blanket to one side, she unwrapped herself and got up. She was still wearing her boots. 'You should have taken them off,' she murmured foolishly.

'I wasn't thinking straight,' he answered blandly.

Not sure what he meant—if, in fact, he meant anything—she gave him another nervous glance. 'Is it all right if I use the bathroom?'

'Yes, of course. I have my own next door. There should be hot water, if the boiler is still working,' he added ruefully. 'Give me five minutes to shower and shave and then I'll make us some coffee.'

She nodded, and, feeling relatively safer standing instead of lying down, blurted, 'Who *are* you, Garde?'

'No one,' he said dismissively.

'Yes, you are,' she argued. 'Nobodies don't have reporters waiting at their gate. Nobodies don't expect innocent gardeners to want to interrogate them.'

'Are you an innocent gardener, Sorrel?'

'Yes!' she insisted.

'Then it could be because of the landing strip I'm allegedly going to build,' he proffered with a rather lazy smile. 'Or—'

'*Landing* strip? Why on earth would anyone want a landing strip?'

'To land planes?' he offered in amusement. 'On the other hand, it could merely be curiosity about why I sold off all my businesses...'

'*All?*' she asked weakly. 'How many did you have?'

'One or two. I'm a very wealthy man,' he added quietly as he carefully watched her face for her reaction. Again, she surprised him.

'Yes,' she agreed absently, 'I supposed you were. If you could afford to buy an abbey.'

'Part of an abbey. Most of it was destroyed during the dissolution of the monasteries.'

'Yes,' she agreed. 'I learned about it in school. And if you're trying to impress me with tales of your wealth, then let me tell you that you didn't succeed,' she added crushingly. 'I'm not impressed *easily*.'

His mouth twitched slightly. 'Go and have your wash,' he ordered softly.

She turned away, and then halted. 'But none of that explains why the reporters hate you.'

'Ah, that's possibly because I confiscated some of their equipment.'

'As in expensive cameras?' she asked as she turned back to face him.

'Mmm.'

'Why?'

'They were being intrusive.'

'Oh. Because of the landing strip?'

'No.' He laughed.

'Then it *could* have been them who uprooted my plants. To get back at you, or something.'

'Could.'

'Then why didn't they uproot your vegetables instead of my plants?' she demanded, feeling outraged all over again.

'I said "could", not "did", and if it was them—which I doubt—they might not have attacked the vegetables because the lower fields are alarmed. I *hate* explaining things.' When she still waited, he sighed. 'A few years ago, before I was here, there had been a spate of horse-thieving. Craddock, the previous owner, who also allowed horses to be kept here, had the lower fields alarmed.'

'Which everyone locally knew about?'

'Yes.'

'But the front garden *isn't* alarmed?'

'No.'

'Then perhaps you ought to think about—'

'Go,' he said firmly.

Pulling a face, she wandered out and padded along to the bathroom next to the room she was supposed to have slept in.

The bathroom still smelled faintly of paint and plaster, and she looked round her at the obviously new white tiles, basin, toilet and corner bath. There was a shower attachment, but no curtain or screen. She closed the door firmly behind her, then hesitated a moment before locking it. Had he been flirting with her? Or merely trying to find out who, what she was? But if he mistrusted her, or thought she had an ulterior motive in being here, which he'd strongly intimated, then why employ her?

Just who *was* Garde Chevenay? And why on earth would anyone think he'd want a landing strip?

Because he had a private plane? He'd said he'd been flying a helicopter... And she couldn't really ask him anything much, could she? Because that was what he seemed to expect, that she would ask questions.

With a little sigh, a bewildered shake of her head, she walked across to stare at herself in the mirror. She looked a wreck. Tilting her head, she stared at the blue swelling on her temple which, for some reason, suddenly encouraged her ribs to ache. Yanking up her sweatshirt, she peered down, gingerly touched them. They felt a bit tender, and there was a red mark just below her heart, but other than that there was no swelling, no sign of a bruise.

Her teeth felt coated, she badly needed a shower, her hands were filthy. But there was no soap, she discovered, no towels. There *was* loo paper. Making do with rinsing her face and hands and drying them on the paper, she smoothed her hair into some sort of order and walked out. She couldn't hear any sounds from Garde's room and so walked downstairs and along to the kitchen.

Garde turned, looked at her, and if she hadn't known him better she would have sworn there was actually a twinkle in his eye. His hair was still wet from his shower, and he was freshly shaven, wearing a clean shirt and grey trousers. She wondered, absently, who did his washing and ironing now that Mrs Davies was away. Or perhaps she came in and collected it.

'You didn't shower?' he asked interestedly.

'No, there weren't any towels,' she said absently. 'Or soap.'

'Oh, hell, I'm sorry…'

'It's all right. I'll have one when I get back to the hotel.' Glancing round her, more to avoid looking at Garde than for any reasons of curiosity, she stared at the piles of rubbish that still sat in the corner, at the dust that hung in the air. 'How long does he reckon it will take?'

'You mean, allowing for the tiles being too large and difficult to cut? The walls not being square? The—'

'OK, OK,' she laughed, 'I get the picture.'

'He's slow, and he complains, but he—eventually—does a good job.' And, of course, more importantly, he was discreet.

'He did the bathroom?'

'Yes. Sugar?'

'Is it coffee?'

'Yes.'

'Then two. Thank you.'

Taking her mug, she said that she would drink hers outside, away from the dust. Without waiting for any reply that might have been forthcoming, she walked out and round to the front, where it was sunny.

Examining the garden, she saw that, thankfully, only two of the turf squares would need replacing, and only one of the shrubs looked terminally ill. The others seemed to have perked themselves up. Hearing Garde behind her, she moved to sit on the step. Garde joined her.

'This is cosy,' he murmured drily, and Sorrel felt her lips twitch.

Leaning back against one of the old doors, she surveyed the garden and felt a feeling of peace steal over her. His closeness wasn't obtrusive now, or alarming, merely comforting.

'It's going to look really nice, isn't it?' she observed.

'Mmm.'

A faint smile in her eyes, she murmured softly, 'Damned with faint praise?'

He glanced at her from the corner of his eye, and then he smiled.

'I haven't seen the little dog lately.'

'He'll turn up,' he said lazily. He's probably got better things to do today.'

'*Why* does he visit?' she asked curiously.

He gave a crooked smile. 'Because Mrs Davies feeds him, I suspect.' When he'd finished his coffee, he got to his feet. 'I'll go and get your truck. Keys?'

Staring up at him almost blankly while she tried to think where she'd left them, she suddenly exclaimed. 'Oh, gosh—they're still in the ignition.'

'Sensible,' he derided.

'Well, I did have other things on my mind!'' she pointed out.

'Mmm.' He put his empty mug on the edge of the skip, cut across the lawn and then climbed over the fence into the orchard.

She watched him, liking the way he moved, remembering how he'd lain beside her earlier, how she'd wanted… Shutting off *that* thought promptly, she determinedly thought about the garden. Whether she would now be allowed to do the back. And whether he would pay her for doing the front *first*.

Moments later she heard the truck start up, and she watched him drive slowly along the lane and across the bridge to park behind the skip. He really was an extraordinarily attractive man. He looked competent and slightly dangerous. A challenge to any red-blooded female.

Shut up, Sorrel.

He climbed out, collected something, locked the door, put the keys in his pocket and held up her torch.

'This yours?'

She nodded.

'I found it in the orchard.' Handing it to her, he added, 'I need to make a couple of phone calls and then I'll drive you to the hotel.'

'I'm perfectly capable of driving myself,' she argued mildly.

'I don't doubt it.' Walking away, he left her to finish her coffee.

'Bossy,' she said, too softly for him to hear. Feeling sleepy and relaxed, she closed her eyes and let the warm sun explore her face, wondering hazily why he'd suspected she was anyone other than who she said she was. Because other people came with false identities wanting to know about him? Know what, precisely? Just who *was* Garde Chevenay?

Hearing the muted rumble of his car engine, she

slowly opened her eyes and watched him manoeuvre carefully past her truck. He halted, threw open the passenger door and waited.

With a little sigh, almost reluctant to move, she put her mug down, got to her feet and joined him in the car.

'I've arranged for us to have breakfast at the hotel. I explained your absence by saying that your truck had broken down.'

'OK.'

'I also rang the police. They're still looking into it.'

'Not a priority, I expect,' she said disgustedly. 'So we still don't know who he was?'

'No.'

'Fingerprints?'

He shrugged.

'They didn't recognise him from the film in the camera?'

'Apparently not, but until he's caught, you will go nowhere without an escort.'

'I...' she began indignantly.

'No buts, Sorrel. I will pick you up each morning, and drive you back to the hotel at night. Unless you want to stay at the house,' he added softly.

'No,' she denied immediately.

'Then you will do as I say.'

Pursing her lips, she stared through the windscreen. 'He probably won't try anything else.'

'Maybe.'

Turning her head, she stared at him. 'Do you *know* what's going on?'

'No,' he stated. 'I don't know *anything*. Do you?'

'No!' she denied.

'Then you will do nothing,' he ordered. 'No night-time adventures, no…sleuthing.' Glancing at her, he waited for her promise. When it wasn't immediately forthcoming, he prompted, 'I want your word, Sorrel.'

'And you'd *accept* it?' she asked with a slight edge to her voice. 'From someone who might not be who she says she is?'

'But you assured me you *are* who you say you are. Didn't you?'

'Yes,' she muttered.

'And is it true?'

'Yes.'

'Then I'll accept your word.'

She hated to have to admit that she wasn't exactly equipped for 'sleuthing', as he put it, especially as she didn't know what was going on, but to surrender her independence…

'Sorrel,' he prompted.

With a little tut, she reluctantly agreed. 'All right, but I don't *like* it.'

'I didn't ask you to.'

He pulled into the forecourt of the small hotel and she climbed reluctantly out. 'How long is this likely to take? Before someone finds him, I mean? Only, once the front is finished…'

'You can start on the back,' he said blandly as he opened the door of the hotel for her.

'That isn't what I meant and you know it!' she protested. 'I shall need transport to go round garden centres—'

'You have transport. Me. Go and have your shower. I'll wait for you in the lounge.'

Collecting her key from the receptionist, who appeared positively *deferential* towards Garde, she went up to her room, feeling grumpy again.

Twenty minutes later she joined him in the dining room and stared at the enormous breakfasts that were placed before them both. 'But I only ever have toast and coffee,' she protested in alarm. She was never going to get through all that.

'Eat,' he ordered.

With a deep sigh, she began. Much to her surprise, she ate it all. 'And don't smirk,' she muttered. Pushing her plate to one side, she poured herself a coffee.

Speaking quietly, he instructed, 'You're to stay in the hotel today, or the grounds. Don't go out.'

'And where will you be?' she asked interestedly.

'Busy. I'll pick you up in the morning at a quarter to eight.' Finishing his coffee, he walked out.

With a little sniff, she poured herself another coffee. When she'd finished, she borrowed a book from the lounge and sat in the garden. Not to read, but to wonder what Garde was up to. Because he was certainly up to something.

*   *   *

He was. When he left the hotel, he called first at the police station, to see what progress, if any, had been achieved, then turned towards Devizes and the home of the man who owned the local paper—and several garages. The sort of man Garde disliked most. Self-important and pompous. Not that he thought the reporter was behind this, but it might be best to make sure.

Half an hour later, he turned off onto a tree-lined road and parked outside the large, ornately imposing detached house. He gave a grim smile when he saw the Rolls Royce ostentatiously parked in front of the double garage. He climbed out, then walked across the expertly paved drive and tugged on the bell-pull. The door was opened by a maid. Unimpressed, he asked to see George Wentsham.

'I'm not sure he's in…' she began worriedly.

He glanced at the car and then back to the maid. 'He went for a walk?' he asked drily. The George Wentsham he knew didn't walk anywhere. Gently taking the door out of her hand, he stepped inside. Glancing derisively round the entrance hall at the showy trappings of wealth, he shook his head. Good taste was one of the things you *couldn't* buy. 'Where is he?'

The maid glanced at a door to her left without saying anything and he smiled his thanks. The maid obviously didn't like him either.

'Claim brutality,' he said softly.

Her lips twitched. 'Shall I sob?'

'You'd do better to leave.'

'Yes,' she agreed. 'I would.'

With a last smile, he walked across to open the door she'd indicated. Closing it behind him, he stared at the overweight man seated importantly behind the desk.

'I said I didn't want to be disturbed—' he began harshly, without looking up.

'Then you should have locked the door,' Garde stated evenly.

Wentsham snapped his head up and stared at Garde with dislike. 'What the hell are you doing here?'

'Looking for information.'

'Then look elsewhere!' he ordered rudely. 'I'm a very busy man. And I do *not* appreciate being disturbed on a Sunday morning.'

'Neither do I,' Garde returned softly. 'I need the address of the reporter who haunts my gate.'

'Then you'll just have to need, won't you?'

Garde just looked at Wentsham, his grey eyes hard. He knew a great many things about George Wentsham, none of them good. And George Wentsham knew that he knew.

Throwing down his pen with disgust, Wentsham retorted irritably, 'We've already been through all that! I told you weeks ago that I'd warned him not to trespass. Which he hasn't,' he added forcefully.

'I didn't say he had,' Garde returned almost mildly.

'Then why do you want him?'

Garde didn't answer.

Leaning back, Wentsham tried to look as intimidating as Garde, and failed. 'Well, he isn't here,' he stated eventually. 'He's covering a gymkhana, the other side of Salisbury.'

'Since when?'

'Friday.'

'Address?'

They stared at each other in silence for long, long moments, and then Wentsham, his mouth tight, suddenly slammed open the right-hand top drawer of the desk and took out a small book. Snapping it open to the appropriate page, he held it out.

Garde ignored it. 'Write it down,' he ordered. 'Together with the name of the place he's staying.'

'I'm not your bloody lackey. Write it down yourself!'

Garde shook his head. Waited. He didn't like intimidation in any form—not from himself, or anyone else—but Wentsham was different. George Wentsham had stepped on the backs of a great many people on his way to wealth without caring what damage he caused, and so Garde had absolutely no compunction at all in using him for his own ends. Garde watched him angrily write down the information and then took the piece of paper that was thrust towards him.

'Thank you.' With a dismissive nod, Garde turned to open the door.

'One day...' Wentsham muttered bitterly.

'Yes,' Garde agreed softly. 'One day. Oh, and George—' he turned back to taunt '—I've been tap-ing the conversation.' With a bad taste in his mouth, he walked out and closed the door quietly behind him.

Sitting in his car, he rang the private investigator on his mobile, gave him the addresses Wentsham had written down and told him what he wanted. Starting the engine, he drove to the house of a home-security company whom he knew very well wouldn't refuse to see him, even on a Sunday. Having money might not impress Sorrel, but it sure as hell had its uses. He then visited the garden centre.

'Who's that?' Sorrel asked, a great deal more suspiciously than she'd intended, as they turned into his drive the next morning.

Deliberately ignoring the elegant young woman who was coming out of his front door, the young woman Sorrel was staring at, Garde glanced at the man crouched down by the bridge. 'Alarm specialist,' he explained briefly and somewhat blandly. 'I took your advice, you see.'

'She's an *alarm* specialist?'

'No,' he denied softly. 'He is.'

Bewildered, she turned to look at him.

He pointed to the crouching man.

'Oh. Then who's...?'

'My accountant. Out you get.'

Wrenching her mind away from the young woman elegantly attired in a business suit, high heels, and with glossy dark hair that was to die for, she climbed out. So did he.

'I bought some replacement turfs yesterday,' he informed her, his expression still bland, 'and removed the damaged ones.'

'So I see.' She also saw that the builder was busy filling up the skip with kitchen rubble. 'Left it a bit late, didn't he? The skip is being picked up this morning.'

'Which is why—' he stated enigmatically.

Glancing at him, and then away again, she frowned.

'Don't worry about it,' he murmured.

'No,' she agreed somewhat blankly as she continued to stand, wait. 'I can't start the drive until the skip's been removed.'

'I know. Replace the turfs then join me in the back garden. We can maybe get a few ideas down on paper.' With a small smile, he went to join the young woman hovering by the front door.

No, Sorrel decided disagreeably, Miss Elegance wouldn't do anything as boring as hover—she was standing *waiting* on the step. And not very patiently, by the look of things. One of those frightfully clever women who could intimidate just by looking.

They spoke briefly, and then she climbed into the natty sports car—that had one wheel on the newly laid turf, Sorrel noticed crossly—and drove past as though Sorrel didn't exist. She nearly mowed down the alarm specialist, before hastily swerving to avoid a postal delivery truck and then roared away into the distance.

Entirely unamused, Sorrel set about replacing the

turf while Garde took possession of, and signed for, a bulky envelope.

Half an hour later the skip was overflowing with rubble. She washed her hands under the outside tap, dried them on her jeans and walked round to find Garde.

He was perched on a broken wall beside a large overgrown privet hedge. Just sitting. His elbows were resting on his knees while he held some papers loosely in his hands. He was staring sightlessly ahead of him. Thinking about his accountant? Who was *more* than his accountant? Perhaps she'd found out that Sorrel had spent a night at the abbey. Perhaps they'd kissed, made up... Shut *up*, Sorrel.

She felt decidedly unlike her normal insouciant self. In fact, she thought disagreeably, she hadn't felt like herself for *ages*, and all because of Garde. She began walking towards him. She didn't see the piece of broken paving because, instead of watching where she was walking, her eyes were fixed on his broad back, on the way his shirt was pulled tight across his shoulderblades, his burned shoulderblades, on the way his thick hair curled across his collar. She caught her foot, lost her balance and, because the paving sloped downwards, fell forwards with a cry of alarm.

Garde turned, half-stood, and held out his arms in a futile effort to stop her falling flat on her face.

CHAPTER SIX

SHE hit him instead, and, even though she was lighter than him, and smaller than him, because he was also off balance his efforts at rescue toppled them both into the hedge.

She didn't say anything, *couldn't* say anything. All the breath had been knocked out of her, so she just stared into his eyes, which were very close to hers. She was lying on his chest, her legs along his, the shrub almost enclosing them; everything seemed to—stop. She made an inarticulate little sound in her throat, but that was all. He didn't make any sound at all, just stared at her as she was staring at him. She could feel every part of him against her, sensitised, aware, and she wanted him.

'No,' she breathed on the ragged edge of panic. She didn't want him. *Couldn't* want him. She'd had enough trouble recently.

She struggled to be free, and he halted her, held her eyes with his, soothed her—and then he kissed her. Gently enfolding her in his arms, he kissed her. The bush they were lying in was springy and large and, without taking his mouth from hers, he carefully rolled her onto her back. He lay on top of her and continued to kiss her. Twigs were sticking into her neck, her back, but all she could feel was his body on hers, his mouth on hers. As though they didn't belong to her, her hands moved to his shoulders, tentatively touched his back as she relaxed into a kiss she hadn't wanted, wasn't prepared for. On a sensible level she knew this was foolish. But in the small part of her that wasn't sensible she knew she had wanted this since the first moment she'd seen him. And it would be all right, wouldn't it? she tried to persuade herself. It was only a kiss.

Kisses, she hazily corrected, that were compulsive and beautiful and exciting. Moreish. With her eyes closed, she inhaled the scent of him into every part of her. Feeling every part of him—the warmth, the heaviness—she continued the soft, greedy exchange.

Pausing for breath, and because he'd heard the skip lorry arrive, he lifted his head and stared down at her flushed face, her swollen mouth, the wide eyes that held a look of bewildered confusion, and he kissed her again. Because he wanted to, because she excited and amused him—intrigued him. She continually surprised him.

'More height differential?' she husked croakily.

'No.'

'It was nice,' she whispered naively.

A smile crinkled his eyes. 'Yes,' he agreed. 'It was. Anything else to say?'

'Say?' she echoed as she continued to stare into his eyes. 'Like what?'

'It's not important. The skip lorry is here.'

'I should say something about the skip lorry?'

His smile deepened. 'No.' Awkwardly groping to

find a solid place for his foot, he levered himself upright and extended a hand to pull her to her feet. 'I think we'll leave the bush, don't you? It might come in—useful.'

She didn't answer, merely looked worried, and a little dazed.

'Don't ask me why, will you?'

She shook her head. She felt shy, which was silly. She'd wanted a flirtation with him… Only this didn't feel like a flirtation, did it? 'I can ask about the first time, though, can't I?'

'Yes,' he agreed softly, 'you can ask about that. Not knowing who you were, not trusting you—because your behaviour was a little bizarre, you must admit—it seemed an easy way of finding out about you.'

'*Kissing* me seemed an easy way?'

'Yes—or, more correctly, your reaction to it was. I wanted to know if you would slap my face, throw your arms round me, or look puzzled, as you did. You also said,' he added, ever more softly, 'that you didn't enjoy it. Didn't you?'

Looking down, away from his eyes that seemed to mesmerise her and make her say things she didn't intend to say, she resolutely kept her mouth closed—and saw that the papers he'd been holding were scattered all across the broken path. She bent to start gathering them up, and he halted her.

'I'll do it,' he said softly.

She rose, allowed the one paper she'd picked up to drop. 'I didn't want this,' she said quietly. 'Didn't want to get involved. I promised Jen I would do my job, not go in the house, get *paid*,' she added wryly.

'There doesn't have to be involvement,' he pointed out.

'No,' she agreed, except that she wasn't sure she could walk away without harm. If there hadn't been an intruder... With a funny little shake of her head, she mumbled, 'I'd better go and pay the skip driver.'

'Yes.' Brushing an errant leaf from her hair, he impulsively kissed her again, just lightly, on her parted mouth. And it wasn't enough, he discovered.

She gave an awkward half-smile and walked towards the front. Everything felt a little unreal. Halting at the corner of the house, she turned to look back. He was watching her. Don't read anything more into it than kissing, she cautioned herself. Because that was all it was. Kissing. And that was all right, because her mind wouldn't move forward anyway. It seemed stuck on those few moments in the bush. And it *was* only a few moments, even though it had seemed like for ever. He'd kissed her because she was—there. And because she gave out the wrong signals? That was what Jen had said. But *were* they the wrong signals? She had *wanted* him to kiss her.

Taking some money from her back pocket, she paid the driver, got a receipt, smiled absently at the builder, who was hovering, and sat on the doorstep to think determinedly about gravel.

*　　*　　*

A strange day, she thought later, as Garde was driving her back to the hotel. She'd barely seen him after the skip lorry had gone. He'd moved both her truck and his car so that she could lay the gravel and then driven off somewhere. And now, sitting beside her, freshly showered and changed, he said nothing. Because there was nothing to say? Because he didn't want to discuss the kiss? And she was more aware of him than she thought she'd ever been aware of anyone in her life.

'Why did you say about the builder only putting his rubble in at the last minute?' she asked, because it was the only thing she could *think* of to ask.

He gave a small smile. 'Because people go through my rubbish,' he said simply.

Staring at him in disbelief, her mouth half-open, she started to say something, frowned, then blurted, 'But *why*? I mean, I know people go through skips to look for—well, useful items, but all there was was—rubble!'

'You can find out quite a lot about people from rubble,' he informed her softly. 'And the only things I ever put out for rubbish are those items that aren't shreddable, like tin cans—and even then they only go out a few minutes before the dustman is due.'

Still staring at him, she finally whispered, 'Who are you, Garde? *What* are you?'

'Paranoid?' he quipped. Pulling up outside the hotel, he switched off the engine and turned to face her. 'Overspill from my famous days.'

'Famous?' she whispered.

'Joke,' he said softly. 'Ever heard of industrial espionage?'

'Yes, of course,' she agreed, still puzzled by his response.

'Then you will know that people who run industries, finance companies, anything remotely sensitive—public figures, the wealthy—are very careful about what they leave lying around. I owned several businesses that might be classed as—sensitive. I don't have them any more,' he added, 'but that doesn't stop people being interested, trying to find out things. I'm also very wealthy.'

'Yes, you said,' she murmured almost dismissively, and he smiled.

'*Very* wealthy,' he insisted. 'I have people knocking on my door looking for hand-outs. I get crank mail, death threats...'

'*Death* threats?' she asked in horror.

'Yes.'

'Then why don't you have minders? More security?' she demanded worriedly.

'Because that isn't how I choose to live. Don't you ever read the newspapers?' he asked in amusement.

'Yes,' she agreed with a frown. 'Not the *financial* pages,' she admitted, 'but—'

'Then that would account for it,' he said drily.

'Are you *laughing* at me?'

'Just slightly,' he confessed. 'It makes a refreshing change not to be—recognised.'

Feeling stupid, a bit out of her depth, she continued to watch him worriedly. 'You expected I would know who you were?'

'Mmm.'

'But I don't.'

'No,' he agreed.

'So tell me.'

He gave a rueful smile. 'I owned a computer firm, a TV production company, a small airline...'

'Landing strip,' she murmured.

'Yes, not that I *want* one here, but...'

'People speculate, start rumours?'

'Yes. I also owned a storage facility, a finance company—'

'Which you sold to the Americans.' She nodded. 'I did know that bit. It was in the article I read at the dentist's. But the other things—' she frowned '—why didn't I know about those?'

'They weren't in my name,' he said simply.

'Oh, but people still obviously knew it was you?'

'Yes. It wasn't a secret.'

Still watching him, trying to come to terms with the fact that he wasn't just wealthy, but—well, mega-rich? she wondered if what he was telling her had been a warning of some kind. As in, I'm beyond your reach so don't get ideas?

'Why did you sell everything off?' she asked curiously.

'Because I got bored. Because I wanted something else to do with my life—and because I was tired of the sort of people I was expected to meet with, socialise with. I like peace and quiet. To be left alone.'

With a rather twisted smile, he added, 'And then I nearly killed myself in a helicopter crash and was nearly gone for ever. I'd already made a start in changing my lifestyle, and lying in a hospital bed only confirmed what I had been feeling for some time. I needed space around me—a period of read-justment, if you like—and so, when I got out of the hospital, I bought the abbey and decided to do it up myself. The press were curious, wanted to know why I had sold everything off. I'm afraid I lost my temper,' he confessed.

'I expect you were in pain,' she said sympathetically.

He gave a small smile. 'Perhaps, but they became ever more intrusive, and when I caught one of them trying to take photographs of the interior of the house, I confiscated his camera and shredded the film. Not very clever, because it only made them the more determined, even more certain that I had something to hide.

'They made up all sorts of stories about me. Speculation that I was ill, had lost my nerve for making money—you name it, they speculated about it. Nothing very much happens round here and so I became a target. They then concluded that the helicopter crash was deliberate, that I was trying to kill myself.'

'That's *terrible*!' she exclaimed.

'Yes,' he agreed, rather amused by her reaction.

'It wasn't sabotage?'

'No,' he denied easily. 'Mechanical fault.'

'People are so—*nosy!*' she burst out.

'Yes.'

Staring at him, seeing his amusement, she murmured, 'Why were you so grumpy, that day I arrived?'

'Oh, bad hair day, I expect,' he quipped. 'The reporters were hovering, I'd had a run-in with Mrs Davies. I went for a walk to calm down and met up with some rather militant ramblers who decided I had no right to keep them off my property, that this was a classless society and that the rich had no right to own land. I'd just finished persuading them to leave when I found the dog stuck down that hole.'

She wasn't sure she believed his glib explanation, but if there *was* another explanation he obviously wasn't going to tell her.

'And then you arrived,' he murmured, 'and I didn't know what to do about you.' Still didn't. The report from the PI, in so far as it went, hadn't linked her with any newspaper, but it *had* linked her with the Right Honourable Nicholas Paignton, and he didn't like that, he found. He wanted her. In fact, he was surprised just how much he *did* want her. But he was still very wary of commitment.

'And you still have no idea who sabotaged the garden?'

'No,' he said with a small frown. 'I went to see the owner of the local newspaper, had someone track down the reporter, but I really *didn't* think it was either of them, and although the owner dislikes me intensely—as I dislike him—whoever did that to the

garden did it out of spite, not dislike. That was petty
revenge. I doubt we will ever know who it was.
Someone you or I slighted, annoyed...'

'There was nothing on the fingerprints, or the car?'

'No, and the car was apparently stolen.' Staring at
her, he added firmly, '*You* are not to investigate.'

With a little twinkle in her eyes, a small smile, she
didn't answer.

'You're causing me enough trouble as it is.'

'Am I?' she asked in surprise. 'Why?'

'Because you aren't like anyone I've ever met.
You intrigue me, irritate me, and amuse me. I also
enjoy kissing you. You have a very nice mouth, Miss
James,' he said softly. 'But an affair with you would
probably be disastrous...'

He said it lightly, but that wasn't how he felt. If
his feelings were just physical, there wouldn't be a
problem—but they weren't, and he couldn't afford
to admit that, even to himself. Gone were the days
of believing people on their say-so, and that was
what he hated the most—not being able to trust without irrefutable proof that he could.

'And who said I *wanted* an affair?' she demanded.

'No one,' he admitted quietly, 'but I'm finding it
increasingly difficult to leave you alone.'

Then don't, she wanted to say, but couldn't, because she didn't know if she could trust her own
judgement. Because of Nick, because of Jen... And
he didn't fully trust, did he? Because he was wealthy,
presumably, and he thought she might be on
the make.

Snapping her eyes away from his, feeling strange and bewildered, she swallowed hard as she tried to make light of it, as he seemed to be doing. 'Now that,' she murmured, 'sounds like something from the last century. Lord of the manor taking a shine to the hired help.'

He smiled. 'It's not in the least like that. And times have changed.'

Yes, but by how much? she wondered. 'When I first met you,' she said seriously, 'I felt all happy. You were so gloriously rude and I wanted to—tease you. And then you kissed me, and everything got a bit muddled. It would have been all right if you hadn't done that.'

'Would it?' he asked gently.

'Yes,' she said not very positively at all. 'I know I'm a bit odd sometimes, and Jen says I give out all the wrong impressions... My life is such a *mess*!'

'Because someone accused you of stealing?' he asked carefully.

'Yes.'

'Tell me.'

'What's to tell? I wasn't prosecuted—which is something, I suppose—but I was blacklisted, unable to get work. I couldn't afford to sue him for defamation of character, or whatever you call it, but I couldn't *prove* he was lying, and so when the work still didn't come in I had to sell the house I'd just bought, sell my car, store all my stuff at Jen's... I didn't really expect you would employ me without a reference. No one *else* had,' she stated, with more bitterness than she'd intended. 'Why did you?'

'So that I could keep an eye on you. Find out what you were up to.'

'But I wasn't up to anything,' she protested.

'No.' Unless it was a spot of blackmail.

'And if I had known you were wealthy, I mean *wealthy* wealthy, I wouldn't have come at all. But when I saw the article, saw the state of the grounds, saw that it was well away from London...'

'Go and have your shower,' he ordered gently.

With a thoughtful sigh, a little nod, she unlatched the door of the car. Walking up to her room without looking back, her mind whirring—so much to think about, worry about—she collected clean clothes and went into the bathroom. What did he want from her? If anything? Had he told her all those things as a warning? But she didn't *need* warning. She'd been blindly naive with Nick; she couldn't afford to make that mistake again.

Droit de seigneur, she thought as she stepped under the shower. The assumption that the master of the house could have anyone he wanted, whether she be serving maid or—gardener? Times had changed, he'd said—which, of course, they had. So why did it still feel like that? If she made any of the first moves, he would think... Not necessarily... Angry with herself, impatient, she snapped off the shower and went to dry her hair.

She put on a dress, then hesitated, wondering if he would think she had put it on for his benefit... Oh, for goodness' sake, Sorrel! Shoving her feet into high-heeled sandals, she slapped on a bit of make-up and went down. Unaware of the rather mutinous expression on her face, she confronted him in the lobby.

'I'm ready,' she announced.

'So I see,' he agreed in some amusement. Taking her arm, he led her towards the front door.

She halted, pulling against his hand. 'The dining room's that way.'

'We aren't using the dining room. We're eating at the abbey. The hotel have kindly prepared a take-away for us. I thought we should celebrate the finishing of the front garden in style.'

Alarmed, wary, she just stared at him. He stared back, his face bland.

Not knowing how to refuse without looking stupid—and, of course, there was the small comfort of knowing that her truck was parked at the abbey, so she could escape if she wanted to—she allowed him to lead her out to his car.

The drive back was made in silence. She couldn't think of a thing to say, and he obviously didn't want to talk. All she *could* think was that Jen was going to be furious with her.

'It's not Jen's life,' she muttered. 'And this is probably a very bad idea,' she announced.

'Why?'

'I don't *know* why,' she denied forcefully. 'If I did, I'd be sitting in the hotel dining room. And where are we to eat?' she added. 'In your study?'

'You'll see.'

He turned into his driveway, and she listened to the satisfying crunch the tyres made on her newly laid gravel.

He stopped the car, climbed out, and went round to open the boot.

With a little sigh, she did the same, and then helped him carry everything into the house.

'Last door,' he instructed.

'That's the refectory.'

'I *know* it's the refectory.'

Walking on, she awkwardly opened the door, and then halted in surprise. The whole room had been transformed. A grouping of four tall wrought-iron candle-holders stood beside the newly cleaned fireplace. A long table with eight chairs sat proudly in the centre of the room, and a small couch had been positioned by the still-uncurtained windows.

'I arranged for the furniture to be installed while I ran you back to the hotel to change,' he explained softly from behind her. 'Can you move? Only these are hot.'

'Oh, yes. Sorry.' Hurrying inside, she put her small box on the table and watched him do the same.

He took a box of matches from the mantelpiece, lit the candles, and then turned to face her. He smiled.   'It's not really dark enough for illumination, but I thought it would give a cheery effect. It is a celebration, after all.'

Moving back to the table, he opened the box she'd been carrying and began to take everything out.

Place-mats, cruet set, knives and forks, glasses, plates, bowls, and a bottle of wine. When he'd laid the table to his satisfaction, one setting at the head of the table and the other to one side, he ordered her to sit while he opened the other boxes.

There was soup to start, kept hot in a flask, followed by chicken and rice in creamy sauce with a side salad, and then fruit and ice-cream, which was beginning to melt.

Still dazed, rather disbelieving, she ate mostly in silence, a silence that was making her more and more nervous. He watched her, and she watched her plate. She would never have said she was a worrying sort of person, but she felt worried now. And why? she wondered. Just because a man says he finds you attractive, it's not a cause for *worry*. It was *nice* to be thought attractive. But she really didn't want an affair. Kissing was all right. She enjoyed kissing him...

'More wine?'

She gave a nervous start and watched him refill her glass without waiting for her answer. She couldn't remember how many glasses that made. Too many, probably. And everything felt charged, electrified. At least, it did to her. He didn't seem to find anything wrong.

'Are you pleased with it?' he asked softly as he pushed the last dish to one side and cradled his wine glass in front of him on the table.

'Pleased?' she echoed with a wary glance at him.

'With the garden.'

'Oh, yes. It needs a few—tweaks,' she murmured,

unable to think of a better word. 'I thought a tall glazed pot by the front door would look nice, bark chippings to suppress weeds, and, of course—'

'Stop babbling,' he reproved, and then added, without change in inflexion, 'I thought platonic for this evening, but I don't think that's to be. Do you? Restrained impulses can get out of hand, don't you think?'

Alarmed, eyes wide, she stared at him. 'I don't have restrained impulses,' she croaked.

'Don't you? Then why are you so nervous?'

'Well, wouldn't *you* be?' she demanded spiritedly.

'No,' he denied with a soft laugh. 'And women aren't usually nervous in my company.'

'Then what are they?'

'Oh, excited, flirtatious...'

'Don't hold your breath,' she muttered, and he laughed. He sounded genuinely delighted, and she scowled at him.

'Perhaps I should marry you,' he quipped gently.

'Yes,' she agreed derisively, 'and perhaps you shouldn't. Is it hot in here?'

'No.' Reaching out, he gently tilted her chin towards him, savoured the feel of her skin beneath his fingers. 'I want to kiss you,' he said softly.

She swallowed hard, felt nervous tension in her stomach, watched his eyes that no longer looked the colour of slate but like warm velvet.

'Want to see round the abbey?'

'Yes,' she agreed hastily. Shoving her chair back, breaking all contact, she got to her feet.

He gave a wry smile. 'Bring your wine with you.'

Mindlessly obeying, needing, wanting to be out of there, out of intimate surroundings that were undermining all her resolutions, she snatched up her nearly full glass and walked to the door. Her footsteps echoed hauntingly on the bare boards.

Taking his time, he got to his feet, picked up his own glass, and joined her.

'Shouldn't you blow out the candles?' Her voice sounded rough, thick, and she coughed to clear her throat.

'They'll be all right,' he dismissed, 'there aren't any draughts in here.' Opening the door, he waited for her to go first. He followed, and the door closed softly, all by itself.

'That's really spooky,' she murmured.

'No,' he denied lazily, 'it's an out-of-true doorframe. This way.' He opened the middle door, and then stood back to allow her through into the narrow stone-flagged passage. And, *because* it was narrow, she was forced to brush against him in order to pass.

Nerves strung tight, tension in every line of her, she walked ahead of him, unbearably conscious of him at her back.

'It used to lead to the chapel,' he informed her softly, and his breath stirred the hair at the back of her neck.

With a little shiver, she hurried on. It was dim here, no windows to shed light. 'Where is it now? The chapel?'

'Gone, like so much else.'

She came to a door on her right and halted uncertainly.

He reached past her and turned the knob, throwing the door wide so that she could enter.

Come into my parlour, said the spider to the fly. Oh, do stop it, Sorrel! She wanted to be in his arms. It was going to happen, she knew it was, and the anticipation, the sheer terror of it, was turning her into jelly.

The room was small, empty, with one wide window overlooking the front garden. 'I'll probably turn it into a small library,' he murmured from so close behind her that she shivered again. He touched her hair and she nearly threw her wine all over herself.

'Now?' he breathed softly.

Feeling strangled, unable to get her breath, she whispered raggedly, 'Now what?'

He grasped her neck through her thick hair with gentle fingers and moved to stand beside her. 'A kiss. It seems to be becoming quite necessary.'

Oh, God.

'Look at me.'

It took her ages to summon up the necessary courage, and, feeling old, worn out, she creakily turned her head. She could only look at his mouth. Which was getting closer, and closer. Shutting her eyes tight, she waited for his kiss and when it happened, when his mouth finally touched hers, she jumped as though she'd been scalded. With an inarticulate little cry, she used her free hand to clutch his shirt-front.

The kiss was urgent, for both of them. His free

hand moved from her hair to her waist, pulled her tight against him, and she slid her own hand up to his neck, forced a closer contact between their mouths.

Her quiet groans and murmurings were unconscious, just soft little sounds in the back of her throat as she exchanged kiss after kiss with him. He tasted of wine. So, probably, did she. And when he lifted his head, took a deep breath, she slowly opened her eyes.

'Better?' he asked huskily.

'No,' she croaked.

Nestling her head against his chest, her hand sliding down to lie against his nipple, she took slow, ragged breaths. She felt his palm smooth her back, from waist to shoulderblade and back again.

'Ready?' he asked, his breath feather-light against the top of her head.

'Ready?' she echoed in breathless bewilderment.

'To continue the tour.'

Surprised, she lifted her head and stared at him. He looked extraordinarily serious. He didn't smile, merely moved his hand to grasp hers and tug her gently out of the room. This door didn't close by itself, and he left it open.

After leading her along the rest of the corridor, until it opened out into a wide stone-flagged square, he halted, turned her to face him and then proffered his wine glass for her to drink from. She obediently did so, and found the small, simple gesture unbelievably erotic.

'I don't know what's happening,' she whispered.

'Seduction,' he told her softly.

'Well, it's definitely working,' she told him equally softly, and he gave a soft, rich chuckle. Unbelievably sexy, unbelievably arousing.

I don't know you, she thought. Dear Lord, I don't know you.

His hand still warmly clasping hers, he led her across the space to a door on the left, then nudged it open with his foot. 'The catch doesn't work,' he explained, for all the world as though nothing had happened between them, as though it really *was* just a tour. 'This will probably be a cloakroom.' Leaning against the doorframe, with her hand still held in his, he tucked her hand behind her back to pull her close and kiss her again.

'How do you feel?'

'Wobbly,' she said promptly, and without thought.

'So do I. The door opposite leads to the cellars. Do you want to look?'

She shook her head.

As they set off once more, he briefly released her hand and opened the door at the far side of the square. Like the refectory, this room was long and wide. There were windows all along the far wall, and wainscoting to waist height on the other three sides, with a narrow ledge, or shelf, above it. Late-evening sun spilled an orange glow across dusty floorboards. 'Swimming pool or games room,' he murmured. 'I haven't decided yet. What do you think?'

'I don't know,' she responded helplessly. Standing

close together in the doorway, his wine glass in his left hand, hers in her right, they both surveyed the dusty scene. His arm was warm against hers, his fingers barely touching her thigh, and all she could think of was that she wanted him. Urgently, desperately. What would he do, she wondered, if she took his glass from his hand, put her own down, and instigated a few kisses of her own? Would he respond? Be amused? What?

Turning her head, she looked up at him, at a stern profile, an unsmiling mouth. A mouth that had touched hers so many times that day. And a feeling of helpless yearning went through her.

As though he'd felt it, as though he knew, he turned his head and looked down at her. His mouth parted slightly and she gave that funny little unconscious groan. She felt warmth spread to her groin, her legs. Her breathing had become unnatural. She shakily groped her glass onto the ledge, then removed his glass and put it with hers. Without taking her eyes from his, or waiting, perhaps, for some sign of disapproval, or otherwise, she slid her hands to his chest, then his shoulders, leaned her body very, very gently against his, closed her eyes, and kissed him.

The warm dryness of his mouth against hers felt electric, and so very necessary. She used her tongue, and felt his body shift, almost unnaturally aware of every breath he took. The warmth of him against her felt somehow hotter, more urgent.

Deepening the kiss, pushing her tongue into his

mouth, she tasted him, sliding her hands into his thick hair and exerting pressure.

His tongue moved to sample hers and she felt his breath accelerate, as did hers, and then, finally, his arms came round her, lifted her against him so that she could feel *all* of him against her through her thin dress.

Shaking, wanting more, she leaned her head back so that he could reach her throat with his mouth. She groaned as one hand lifted the hem of her dress and pressed warmly against her bare thigh, to hold her more securely against him.

She could feel his arousal and it excited her. Could feel his hot palm through her thin panties. Eyes tight shut, head still back, so that her hair fell in a curtain almost to her waist, breathing ragged, she clutched his shoulders tight, gritted her teeth to contain the need as his mouth sucked greedily against her throat. It was frightening and exciting. She had never felt like this, never wanted anyone as much as she now wanted him, and she thought she would die if fulfilment wasn't forthcoming.

He lifted his mouth, took a deep, shuddering breath, and slowly allowed her to slide downwards until her feet reached the floor. Head back against the doorframe, his own eyes closed, he held her gently within the circle of his arms.

When he had his breathing under control—his emotions, if not squashed, at least held marginally in check—he gently moved her so that he could look down into her face. He wanted her. Dear God, how he wanted her, and he was so tired of pretence. 'It's not enough, is it?' he asked huskily.

'No,' she managed. And it wasn't going to go away. She knew that. Now.

'We could stop here, end it here, but—'

'We would always wonder,' she finished for him, 'and maybe regret.'

'Yes.' Absently smoothing her tumbled hair, enjoying the silky feel of it, enjoying and being aroused by the feel of her fingers against his chest, he asked, 'An affair, then?'

'Sounds awfully clinical put into words,' she murmured as her eyes continued to be held by his.

'I don't feel clinical.'

'Neither do I.'

'What do you see?' he asked softly.

'A man.'

'Who?'

'Has the ability to turn my emotions inside out. Jen is going to be *furious*.'

He gave a faint smile. 'Why?'

'Because she made me promise not to get involved.'

'Was it a likelihood?'

She gave a wry, rather shaky smile. 'I didn't think so, but...'

'But?'

'She could tell by my voice that I liked you. Was—interested. In a flirtation,' she added quickly. 'She says I have terrible judgement.'

'And do you?'

She sighed. 'I don't know. I tend to believe in people. What do you see?' she asked curiously as she flattened out her palms and began to rub them rhythmically against his chest.

His smile turned crooked. 'A young woman who seems to be disordering my life. A young woman I should probably never have kissed because now the kisses matter.'

'Do they?' she asked, her voice soft and weak.

'Yes.' And still he tried to refute the possibility that this was more than attraction.

Moving one hand up to his chin, she exerted gentle pressure to part his lips, and felt that funny dip in her stomach again, the warmth in her groin. Eyes on his parted mouth, she murmured, 'I wasn't sure if I should touch you, didn't know if the first moves had to come from you, but now—dear God, Garde,' she added thickly, 'I didn't think it was possible to feel so wanton. Is it what you want?'

'Yes,' he agreed, and his voice was as thick as hers, and he discovered, not at all to his chagrin, that his arousal wasn't in check at all.

CHAPTER SEVEN

HE CONTINUED to examine her face. When he'd first seen her he hadn't found her pretty at all. Now, he found her almost beautiful. She had the loveliest eyes, bluey green with a dark ring round the iris. Her mouth was full, extremely kissable. She had freckles on her nose, and he wanted very badly to make love to her. 'Wouldn't it be nice if I could conjure up a bed? We could lie in the dying sunlight...' With an abrupt movement that took her by surprise, he straightened—forcing her to do the same—took her hand in a brisk fashion that made her start, and tugged her back to the refectory. The candles still burned brightly in their sconces. They seemed so much brighter because the late sun didn't reach this part of the house.

Leaving her at the doorway, he strode across to blow them out and then returned to her side. In the dim light he looked different—darker, larger, more exciting—as he took her hand again and led her towards the shadowy staircase.

She needed no urging to climb or follow him along to his room. Her breathing was erratic, and she felt light-headed. Her nerves had been dispelled, but not her anticipation, her need. Her whole body ached with wanting him. Wanting to know what it was like to lie with someone who made you feel weak, out of control.

He didn't put on the light, merely quietly closed the door and led her over to the bed. And then he stopped. Shadows gave the room mystery, heightened tension and awareness. Electricity crackled between them as they stood still, close, but no longer touching, and the longer they stood the more aware they became, until slowly, like a sleepwalker, she began to unbutton her dress. She allowed it to slip to the floor with a sensuous whisper of fabric, and then waited for him to undo his shirt.

It seemed to take a very long time to undress, item by item, person by person, first her, then him, until all that was left were her high-heeled sandals.

The room felt charged as he finally reached out and ran one warm finger down between her breasts to halt at her navel. She shivered and lifted her hands to touch his nipples, rub her thumbs across the peaks. But the feel of his warm flesh was too much for mere touching and she stepped closer, so that her breasts touched against him and so that his arousal could brush against her.

Her throat felt too thick for words and so she held him, touched him, revelled in the feel of him against her. She tried to breathe normally, tried not to be hasty, grab, urge, but it was so hard, and so unlike how she'd thought she was.

This is Garde Chevenay, she kept telling herself. The one man she wanted above all others. A man who was probably way out of her league. A man who excited her, whose kisses made her feel weak, urgent. And she didn't want him just for sex, not just for fulfilment or excitement, but because she liked him, wanted to—love. Snapping her eyes open in shock, she stiffened, and he immediately halted his own exploration.

'Sorrel?' he queried softly, his voice a husky murmur in the dark.

Love? Oh, good heavens. Was that how it happened? Trundling along, not knowing that it was happening, until, all of a sudden, you—loved? No.

'Sorrel?'

'What? Sorry,' she whispered. 'I…' Staring into his face, examining it, really looking at it feature by feature, she knew that he wasn't like Nick. That he really, really wasn't, but… No, she wouldn't allow Nick to spoil this, like he had spoiled everything else. She wouldn't. Slowly raising her hands, barely aware that she did so, she traced each contour of his face with her fingertips.

'What is it? You want to stop?'

'No,' she denied, 'but I just suddenly realised the enormity of it all.'

'Define enormity,' he persuaded softly.

'I can't,' she said helplessly. 'It feels so big, so— encompassing, and I just realised that I want this more than anything.'

'And it frightened you?'

'Yes.' Because she was so very afraid that she might be wrong about him. As she'd been wrong once before about Nick. She'd liked Nick; she'd trusted him. She hadn't wanted to make *love* with him, but... 'Do you think I'm silly?'

'No, and if you want me to stop—at any time,' he emphasised.

'I know.'

'Do you?'

'Yes.' She did know that. She *did*. She knew that Garde would never force her, or be angry. She had to believe in herself, otherwise life wouldn't be worth living. 'I feel as though I know you very well,' she whispered. 'Isn't that strange?'

'Spooky,' he said softly, and she saw the gleam of his teeth as he smiled.

Smiling back, she wrapped her arms around him again, snuggled close and inhaled the scent of him. She would believe in him, and herself. She had to. 'This is so beautiful,' she said softly. 'How odd not to even feel nervous, as though...' As though they belonged. She tried to tell herself not to be stupid, but the thought wouldn't go away until he touched her intimately and then it did go away, to be replaced by other thoughts far more erotic and exciting than belonging.

'Horizontal would be nice,' he whispered against her ear, and she gave a throaty chuckle.

'Go ahead. I have to take off my shoes.'

He released her, then lay on his side in the middle of the wide bed, head propped on his upraised hand, and watched her bend to take off her sandals. When she straightened, light from the window caught her to show him her shape, the perk of her small breasts, the narrow waist and soft flare of hips a boy would be proud to own. Slim, and yet somehow sexy, with legs that went on for ever, she sat on the side of the bed, swung her feet up and lay beside him.

'Can you not lie on your back?' she asked softly as she began to trace his mouth with one finger.

'Can. Don't want to.'

'Because it's still painful?'

'Not painful, no. More…sensitive. How are your aches and pains?'

'Not too bad.' She'd taken the plaster off her temple and, although her ribs were still tender, there were no obvious bruises. 'Certainly not bad enough to prevent—'

'Good.' He rested his hand on her hip, began to knead her soft flesh.

Watching him watching her, she said thickly, 'Let me know if I hurt your back.'

'I will. It doesn't bother you?'

'The scarring?' she asked softly. 'No.'

'Good.' Without haste, he leaned forward until his mouth could touch hers, flirt with it using tongue and teeth. His hand slipped further to her rear, causing her to drag in a sharp breath and then release it as she moved her hand to his hip, mimicked the moves he was making.

He groaned, parted her mouth more urgently and pressed his fingers deeper into her flesh, fingers that were experienced, sensitive, until she almost cried out with the sensation after sensation that assailed her. He was aware of her in a way that surprised him, already getting used to the rush of feeling she generated whenever she was near, but it still took his breath away when she did to him what he was doing to her. Used to being dominant, bored, he admitted honestly, he took pleasure in submission.

It seemed to go on for a very long time as they explored each other with a thoroughness that brought peak after peak of pleasure, until, finally, neither could wait any longer for ultimate fulfilment.

Exhausted, satiated, they lay entwined in the rumpled bedcover. She eventually stirred and began to trace one finger across his strong chin. She wasn't sure she believed all that had happened.

'How did we come to this so quickly?' she wondered.

'From bush to bed?'

She smiled. 'I was quite determined not to get involved.'

'So was I, but even in the beginning you intrigued me. You aren't like anyone I've ever met. I'd watch you digging about in the dirt, and I'd want you. With every moment that passes I can feel myself being drawn deeper and deeper.'

'And you resent it?' she guessed.

'No,' he denied in surprise. 'Why on earth would I resent it?'

'I don't know. I suppose I sort of assumed that men did. Being out of control and all that macho thing.'

He gave a small laugh. '*What* macho thing? There are a few men—and it is only a few, I think—who behave with idiotic dominance, as though their images will suffer if they don't, but most of us take pleasure in being with a beautiful woman.'

'But I'm not. Beautiful, I mean. Your accountant is beautiful.'

'And absolutely terrifying. Another one who's full of misconceptions about the male psyche. She talks to me as though I'm four.'

'Intellectually challenged?' she grinned.

'Something like that. I also think that perhaps you're rather beautiful inside.'

Astonished, flattered, and really rather humbled, she didn't know quite what to say. She shook her head. 'No,' she denied. 'I could be much nicer. I sometimes—'

He put his fingers over her mouth. 'Don't deride it.' He didn't want her to tell him what made her not very nice. Not now. The thought of Nicholas Paignton rose in his mind and he hastily squashed it.

She gave a funny little smile, and murmured, 'That was a nice thing to say.'

'Was it? And don't people usually say nice things to you?'

'I don't know,' she confessed. 'Sometimes. Someone once said I always smelled nice. Although I don't suppose I do when I've been working all day.'

'Does anyone?' He chuckled. 'Sleepy?'

Thinking about it, she shook her head again. 'No, which is somewhat surprising, seeing as we didn't get very much sleep the other night—or even tonight. Lazy—but, no, not sleepy.'

'Then perhaps I ought to fetch the wine we didn't finish. Now that I don't have to drive you back to the hotel, I can have some more.'

'Sounds good.'

He dropped a kiss on her nose and rolled to his feet. His back might not be painful any more, but he still favoured it, kept it away from contact with the bedding, or even his chair, she remembered.

Lying back, snuggling into the cover, she stared at the window, tried to examine her feelings. She tried to think ahead, and couldn't. And *why* was she trying to think ahead? she wondered. Because that was what women did? Why couldn't she just enjoy the moment? Because Jen was forever telling her she should look to the future, think about repercussions, security, and while that was all very well when it came to pensions, savings, why did it have to involve feelings? She wasn't *like* her sister, and so she really shouldn't try to live her life the same way. Her judgement *wasn't* screwed. Well, maybe it had been in that one instance.

Jen was a carer, seemed to have the need to look after people. She had found true fulfilment in being a wife and mother, which was fine—for Jen. But Sorrel didn't think she was made of the same stuff. She didn't yearn to get married, have babies—or not yet, anyway. She would probably change, of course, but at the moment all she wanted was to enjoy herself, have plenty of work and enough money to live.

So why keep trying to query what was happening with Garde? Why not just enjoy? He wasn't thinking of the future, of commitment—she knew that very well. This was an—affair. An affair he'd thought about for some time, if his earlier words could be believed, which only meant that he'd been being cautious. As she had.

She heard his footsteps on the stairs, and turned her head to watch him enter. She *liked* him. Enjoyed being with him. She wanted to take pleasure in his body, and it was a *beautiful* body, she noted as he walked towards her carrying the wine bottle and their glasses. Strong legs, flat stomach, a wonderfully muscular broad chest. She also wanted him to take pleasure in hers. What was so wrong with that? And if she felt she belonged, then fine—enjoy the belonging for however long it lasted. She really mustn't use Jen's yardstick for things. She had to make her own mistakes, take her own pleasures.

He smiled at her. 'Come on. Up,' he urged softly, and she grinned.

Hoisting herself up in the bed, tucking a pillow behind her, she took the bottle of wine from him. Entirely unashamed of her nakedness, her rather rangy form, she tucked the bottle against her side, then yelped at its coldness and took the glass he was holding out.

'This feels delightfully decadent,' she teased.

'Well,' he drawled as he settled himself beside her, 'if it's decadent you want...' Tilting his glass, he tipped a very small amount of wine across her tummy.

'Garde!' she protested, laughing as the liquid began to run to either side of her. 'I shall end up lying in a puddle!'

'No, you'll end up being licked.'

With that squirmy feeling in her tummy, she looked at him a bit uncertainly.

'Not quite ready for decadence?' he queried gently.

'Not quite,' she agreed. 'Is that what you like?' she asked hesitantly.

'I like whatever you like.'

'I don't know what other things I like,' she said with a seriousness that made him smile. 'Yet,' she added.

Clinking his glass against hers, he toasted softly, 'Here's to learning.'

'And to my teacher?' she asked.

'To your teacher,' he agreed.

He was a very good teacher. Certainly he taught her a lot of things she didn't know, and over the next week they grew even closer. And yet, she was often aware of a barrier between them. Because it was an affair, she tried to tell herself. But she knew it wasn't just that. He would be distant sometimes, thoughtful, and then he would smile and it would be all right again.

Perhaps it was that she was still cautious herself, waiting for him to change, the way Nick had changed. Perhaps that was all it was. Perhaps *he* was still cautious.

She didn't move into his house—not entirely, anyway. She spent most of her nights with him, and obviously her days, because she was working. There was no further sabotage, even though the police hadn't yet found the man who'd done it, and she felt happier than she had in a very long time. There was a kind of excitement in going back to the hotel each evening to shower and change, eat their meal. Sometimes he waited in her bedroom whilst she showered, sometimes he joined her, and sometimes he waited downstairs in the lobby. The hotel staff must have known what was going on, but neither by look nor deed did they ever refer to it. There were no smirks or suggestive looks, just acceptance that that was how things were.

She would then collect her work clothes for the next day and they would drive back to the abbey. Sometimes they would sit in the rear garden to enjoy the light summer evenings and discuss what she was doing, what plants he would like. They talked about music, art, lightly touched on politics, how his vegetables were growing, his improvements to the house progressing, and one evening he took her on a tour of the surrounding countryside. They passed Stonehenge, where crowds would gather for the summer solstice; Woodhenge; drove through local towns.

By Friday, the kitchen had a decent floor, a sink, a washing machine, dishwasher and oven. She refused to think what would happen when the garden was finished.

He also refused to think about it. He also kept thinking about Nick. He didn't *want* to, but, like a spectre at the feast, Nick always seemed to be there. Garde didn't know if she'd had an affair with him, and wouldn't ask. He didn't want to know. Yes, he did. The initial report from the investigator had mentioned theft, which she'd told him about. It had also mentioned blackmail. And tomorrow he would know the truth. Would get the final report on her. He felt guilty, and a heel, but he needed to know.

The weather stayed fine and so Sorrel wore her cut-off jeans the next day. She didn't think she looked entirely wonderful in shorts, with her long slender legs, but she didn't care. She knew Garde sometimes watched her from a window, or from the terrace, and, instead of feeling awkward or self-conscious, she found that she revelled in it.

Dirty and sweaty at the end of each day, she felt content—nearly content. She didn't know what she needed for full contentment; she only knew that it wasn't yet achieved. Brushing aside her doubts, which Jen would no doubt have called her being short-sighted, she continued with the work that always made her so truly satisfied.

Even a visit from his stunning accountant didn't mar her pleasure.

Garde had nipped out, for something unspecified, and she was marking out the perimeters of the par-

terres by dribbling soft sand in intricate patterns that
would soon be planted with the box hedging she'd
had to order especially, because it was quite difficult
to get. Sorrel didn't even hear the accountant arrive.
Instead she gradually became aware she was being
watched. She straightened, slowly turned, and smiled
at the stunningly attractive young woman.

'No greater contrast,' Sorrel murmured on a laugh
as she looked down at her dirty knees, her stained
shorts and her filthy hands.

'No,' the woman agreed, without a flicker of hu-
mour. 'Is Garde about?'

'He popped out for a few minutes. He shouldn't
be long. Or, if you don't want to wait, you could
leave a message with me if you like.'

The woman looked Sorrel up and down, in a really
rather insulting kind of way, then gave a slight shake
of her head. 'I don't think so.'

Amused, Sorrel asked softly, 'Because I'm a gardener?'

'Because I doubt you would understand the message,' she murmured. 'No insult intended, but—'

'Accountants are clever and gardeners—are not?'

'Not in my experience, no. But then, I could no
more plant up gardens,' she stated somewhat dis-
tastefully, 'than you could—'

'Account?' Sorrel put in. 'You shouldn't make
snap judgements, Miss...?'

'Wild.'

Sorrel hastily bit her lip. Now *there* was a mis-
nomer if ever she'd heard one. 'But you're probably

right,' she murmured. 'I don't really know very much about high finance.'

'No,' Miss Wild agreed, as though it really came as no surprise.

'I can do my sums, and I was quite good at English and History at school, but...' Wanting very badly to laugh, because she could have added that she had a degree in both, Sorrel asked, 'Do you want to wait inside? I could get you a cup of coffee if you like.'

Miss Wild glanced at Sorrel's hands, and shuddered. 'No, thank you. I'll wait in the car.' Turning carefully on her elegant high heels, she walked slowly round the side of the house.

A wide smile on her face, Sorrel picked up her bag of sand. No, she really couldn't see the elegant Miss Wild grubbing about in the earth. She would break her nails, for one thing. Glancing at her own short and currently very dirty nails, she grinned.

A few minutes later she heard Garde's car pull in and, not long after, the throaty roar of Miss Wild's engine as she departed.

'Not one for long visits, is she?' she observed when Garde strolled round to join her. He was carrying a long brown envelope and looked extraordinarily happy.

'What?' She smiled.

'Nothing. Have a nice little chat with her, did you?'

'Mmm.' Eyes sparkling with mischief, she pressed a grubby kiss on his mouth. 'And it's a crying shame that a woman that pretty should be so humourless. Does she know about us?'

'Not from me. Why?'

'Because, if she did, I think her opinion of your intellect would hit rock bottom.'

'It's already rock bottom. Perhaps I should tell her about your degr—I like the sand,' he added quickly as he glanced behind her. 'Very avant-garde. Clever little puss, aren't you?'

'Yes,' she agreed smugly. 'Where did you go?'

'Out,' he said promptly, and then he pulled her to him and kissed her warmly on the mouth. Warmly and passionately, and somehow gently.

Surprised—pleased, but surprised—she searched his face. 'You seem—different.'

'I am. Come and talk to me,' he persuaded softly.

'Now?' she asked, puzzled.

'Mmm.'

Head on one side, she searched his face. 'Is it important?'

'I think so.'

'Can I just finish this?'

He gave a wry smile that she didn't understand. 'If you must. But don't be *long*.'

'No,' she agreed weakly as she watched him walk back towards the house. With a bewildered little shake of her head, she went back to her patterns. What had made him different? The letter he was carrying? Or the news Miss Wild had brought? Thinking about her, she gave a little chuckle. Perhaps he would tell his accountant about her degrees next time they met...

Halting abruptly, unaware that her sand was spilling out into an uncontrolled mound, she frowned. She hadn't told him about her degrees, so how had he known? He had definitely been going to say 'degrees', and then he'd quickly mentioned her sand to cover it up. And kissed her.

Straightening, with the empty bag in one hand, the other on her aching back, she stared blindly towards the end of the garden. She *hadn't* told him; she knew she hadn't. Half turning towards the house, as though to confront him, she saw the pile of sand, and cursed. Squatting, she began to scoop it back into the bag. She'd confront him later, when they had their talk—whatever *that* was about. He hadn't looked serious, or solemn—more sort of...well, happy.

Continuing all round the garden, hurrying now, periodically consulting the sketch she'd made, she continued to puzzle over it. Perhaps he'd spoken to Jen, she mused. Jen could have rung for something... Not that he usually *answered* his phone, just left the answering machine on, but he *could* have spoken to Jen, and it *could* have come up in conversation. Jen did like to boast that her sister had a brain, and had 'wasted' it by going into horticulture.

Unaware of her frown, she walked slowly round to the other garden and tossed her empty bag on the growing pile of rubble by the greenhouses. On the other hand, if he knew a private detective... Stopped in her tracks, she stared ahead of her. He'd had her investigated, hadn't he?

So? she asked herself. What was there to find? Nothing. Except that she'd been blacklisted, and he knew about that. And wouldn't you investigate someone who didn't have references? she asked herself. Possibly, but he might have *told* her.

Slowly retracing her steps, still thinking about it, she wasn't sure whether to be angry or not. She bent to turn on the outside tap near the utility room door. Hearing voices, she glanced curiously towards the front garden, and then stiffened in shock.

Garde was standing on the gravel—talking to Nick.

CHAPTER EIGHT

HER first thought was denial. It couldn't possibly be
Nick. He didn't know where she was. Unless Garde
knew him, and had told him...

Slowly straightening, she continued to stare until
a fury so sudden and so immediate erupted through
her that she felt momentarily faint. Without thought,
just sheer, unbridled anger, she strode towards the
slim, fair-haired man, with her mouth set, her face
hard—and hit him as hard as she could across the
face.

'Get out!' she grated. Shoving at his shoulders,
pushing him backwards, she continued both verbal
and physical assault. 'How dare you come here with
your sneaky, despicable little ways? How *dare* you?'
she yelled, and the expression of astonishment on his
face would have been comical if she had been in any
mood to be amused.

'I...'

'Shut *up*!' she screamed as her furious advance
forced him into a rearwards shuffle. 'This is *it*! End
of story! *Finis!* There will be no more screwing up
of my life, and if I get so much as even a hint of
you following me or having me followed, I'll sue
you for harassment! I *should* have sued you for defamation of character! Taken you to court for your

155

lies and manipulation! God knows why I didn't! You are *pathetic*!'

Almost at the bridge, still shoving at him, she probably looked like a wild-haired, filthy virago. She was so angry that the words were bubbling out of her without thought or reasoning. 'You are a deceitful, cowardly, self-important little prig,' she spat. 'With no more idea of proper behaviour than a toad! In fact, you *are* a toad! A sneaky, inadequate, loathsome little toad! Wealth doesn't give you the right to ride roughshod over people; *nothing* gives anyone the right to do that! You are arrogant, stupid, illinformed. You don't even have the wit to see how people regard you. You don't see the *sniggers* at your posturing! You're a little man who thinks women should fall at your feet and be grateful they've been noticed! A little man who thinks everyone can be bought! Well, I've got news for you,' she continued breathlessly as she forced him right out into the lane. 'Right Honourable Nicholas Paignton, who has absolutely no honour at all, you are *despised*! Now go away and don't you ever come near me again! Not *ever*!'

Turning, she strode back the way she had come. Just walked and walked until she came up against the barrier of the rear gate and then stood with her hands clenched on the bars as though she were imprisoned. How dared he? How *dared* he?

Shaking so badly she felt ill, her eyes blurred with angry tears and her breath coming in laboured gasps, she stared blindly at the horses on the far side of the field. It was Nick who'd ruined the garden, wasn't it? Nick who'd employed someone to pull up the plants, muck up the lawn...

She heard Garde's footsteps behind her and tightened her grip on the bars. 'Don't say *anything*,' she hissed. 'Don't say anything at *all*!'

He didn't.

Leaning her forehead against the gate, she took in a shuddering breath. 'What did he tell you?' she demanded bitterly. 'In his soft, hesitant, little-boy voice, of course, that fools *everybody*? That I was a good-time girl? That I stole from him? That I promised to marry him and then turned him down in front of his friends? Or that I'm a little whore who...' Slamming her hand angrily against the metal, she gritted, 'He is *despicable*.'

'He said he thought you were probably a professional thief,' he said, really quite mildly.

'Yeah, right,' she agreed scathingly. 'And I bet he was all diffident and apologetic—so sorry to trouble you, but he thought it was his duty, blah, blah, blah. I *hate* him!' she grated.

'Yes, I imagine you do,' he agreed quietly.

'I could write a *book* about him!' she continued fiercely. 'I could verbalise for *years* about his perfidy.' Unable to stop the tears that were running down her grubby face, she wiped them angrily away with the back of her hand.

'He also said,' he continued in the same quiet voice, 'that he was completely taken in by your apparent sincerity, your hard work. He also admitted that you were a very good gardener.'

'Nice of him,' she grated.

'And that you teased him, made him laugh, and that you thought an affair with him would be very nice. He admits he was naive, foolish, but it never even occurred to him that you would want more than an affair, that you would want property, money…'

'Oh, yes, I'm a *blackmailer*, aren't I?' she said sarcastically. 'I wonder what it was I found out in order to be one. Did you invite him? Do you know him?'

'No.'

'Then how did he find out where I was?'

'A photograph was taken of you, remember?'

'How could I forget?' she derided angrily. 'And he peruses every local paper he can get his hands on, does he? Every county, every town…'

'It was apparently printed in one of the glossy magazines.'

'Was it?' she asked bitterly. 'Wow.' It was a wonder Jen hadn't picked up on it. 'But you did have me investigated, didn't you? So you could have met him.'

'Could have,' he agreed. 'Didn't.'

'And do you now think I was out to blackmail you?' she demanded. 'How fortunate he came. Boy, did you have a lucky escape.'

'Sorrel…' There was an anguished shout from the kitchen and he broke off, turned swiftly, then broke into a run as the builder continued to yell with a great deal of urgency.

Left shaking by the gate, unable to move for the moment, even if she'd wanted to, she took another shuddering breath. Could have. Didn't, she repeated numbly to herself. So he had known about Nick all along, hadn't he? Or maybe not *all* along. How long did it take sleuths to sleuth? She had no idea. And what did it matter anyway? Nick had done his work, made his mischief. But had he been believed? He usually was, she thought bitterly. Oh, yes, he usually was. And he and Garde were of the same school, weren't they? Wealth, privilege. Men like that stuck together, believed each other. She really didn't want to stand here and wait for Garde to come back, only to be interrogated. Why should she? If he'd cared for her, *really* cared for her, he would have held her, comforted her.

Without haste, without very much feeling, she released her grip on the gate and walked shakily down the track she'd marked out for the path. She glanced into the kitchen as she passed, saw that the stepladder had slipped and now lay drunkenly against the wall, saw that both Garde and the builder were awkwardly supporting a large cupboard, and carried on towards the front.

Her keys were in the truck, and so she climbed in, turned on the ignition, and drove away. She thought she heard him shout, but that might have been her imagination. She couldn't hear anything very clearly over the sound of the engine.

She didn't know where she was going. Didn't care. She didn't want to think or plan. She just wanted to be by herself. Her tears drying on her dirty face left white streaks, but she was unaware of them, uncaring. She drove for miles, her mind spinning frantically. Why had she left it until now to attack Nick? Why hadn't she done it months ago? Why on earth had she been so inept? Because she'd been hurt, unable to think clearly? Or because pride had got the better of her? She'd told herself she didn't care, that people could believe what they wanted to believe, so why was now different? Because of Garde. Because it mattered. Because she was in love with him.

With a bitter laugh, she pulled over to the side of the road, switched off the engine and rested her forehead on the steering wheel. Eyes open, she stared blindly down. In love with. Define love, he would have said, if she'd told him—which she hadn't, because it was an affair, not a romance, or a commitment... She hadn't wanted marriage, or children....Liar, liar, liar, she scolded herself. You tell yourself things, Sorrel, and you make yourself believe them. She did love him. She thought she loved him very much. And she wanted him to love her back. That was why she'd held back, been cautious, because *he* only wanted an affair.

Screwing her eyes tight shut, she tried to stop the tears, and then jumped visibly when her mobile rang.

Groping it off the parcel shelf, she automatically answered it.

'Sorrel? It's Jen!' She sounded vibrant, alive, excited. 'You didn't tell me he looked like *that*.' Not waiting for Sorrel to answer, she rushed on, 'Boy, no wonder you were interested.'

Confused, frowning, Sorrel mumbled, 'What?'

'*Garde!*'

'Garde?'

'Yes! Are you all right?' Jen asked belatedly. 'Only you sound...'

'No, I'm fine,' Sorrel said dismissively. 'I just don't know what you're talking about.' Had Garde been sneaking about behind her back? Meeting her sister, Nick...?

'Garde!' Jen repeated impatiently. 'I was re-reading the article you asked me to find and it mentioned a spread in a magazine, one of those expensive glossies, and I suddenly thought I'd probably got it! You know I always buy those glossy magazines! Are you still there?'

'Yes,' Sorrel agreed.

'Anyway, I had a hunt through the spare room—and I found it!' Jen added triumphantly. 'Boy, was I relieved.'

'Relieved?' Sorrel echoed weakly.

'Yes! No way would someone like that be interested in you! And I had been worried, I must admit, but now that I've seen what he looks like, seen the sort of women he goes out with! He was with Verena McCoist! Apparently they're an item. Or were.'

Voice even weaker, Sorrel whispered, 'Verena McCoist?'

'Yes! The model! Top model,' she emphasised. 'He's a multi-millionaire, Sorrel!'

'Yes, I know.'

'Knee-weakeningly sexy, isn't he?'

'Yes.'

'And that *smile*. So, I was relieved,' Jen continued happily, 'that there wouldn't be any involvement. Men like that do *not* go out with gardeners.'

'No.' But they did have affairs with them.

'So what's he like?'

'Nice,' Sorrel said inadequately.

'Well, let's hope he's also generous. Has he paid you yet?'

'No, not yet.'

'Sorrel! I told you. Money up front.'

'Yes, I know you did.'

There was a little pause, and then Jen asked worriedly, 'Are you sure you're all right? Only you sound a bit strange.'

'It's not a very good connection,' Sorrel fabricated. 'Look, I have to go; I'm in the truck.'

'Oh, OK. Ring me later.'

'OK. Bye.' Disconnecting, Sorrel stared blankly through the windscreen. Men like that... But he wasn't like that, was he? He might be now, after she'd shown herself up as a little virago. He probably wasn't used to women behaving like that.

She'd amused him for a while, hadn't she? Because she was different. But, as Jen had said, men like that didn't have permanent relationships with girls like her, did they?

Nick had wanted to... Nick was a pillock. Taking a deep, shaky breath, she put the mobile back on the shelf. And even if by some miracle Garde *didn't* mind her behaving like a fishwife, and did believe her and not Nick, he didn't want her love, did he? He wanted an affair. Which he was having. Or had had. If he'd cared for her, believed in her, he would have hugged her, told her it was all right—not calmly recited all the things Nick had said, as though he had already known them.

When had he got the report on her? she wondered. Before he'd told her all about himself? Probably before he'd kissed her in the bush. Until he'd discovered he could trust her, he wouldn't have kissed her, would he?

She shouldn't have run away. She should have waited until the drama in the kitchen had been resolved, confronted him, and then she would have known. One way or the other. She felt sick, but she had to go back, didn't she? Even if it was only to get the money she was owed.

Turning on the engine, she did a quick U-turn and began driving back the way she had come. Or the way she thought she had come. It took her two hours, and when she *did* arrive it was to find that Garde had gone out. The builder didn't know where.

'Are you all right?' he asked quietly.

'Me? Yes, I'm fine,' she said listlessly. 'Are you?' she finally remembered to ask. 'I'm sorry I didn't wait around to see what the emergency was. I was—'

'Upset. Yes,' he agreed awkwardly. 'I heard the commotion out front.'

'Hard not to, I imagine,' she said bitterly. 'Well, if Garde comes back, I'll be at the hotel getting cleaned up—' No, she suddenly decided. She was going to stay here. Finish what she'd started. This time she *wasn't* going to run away. If he wanted her to go, then he would have to say so. 'I'll be here,' she substituted quietly.

'OK, but I should, um, wash your face first.'

Smudging her hands across it in reflex action, she gave a small grimace and went to sluice it under the tap.

This is stupid, she told herself as she walked round to the rear. You might just as well leave the garden as it is. She was probably out of a job; definitely out of an affair…. *You don't know that.* Yes, she did. But if she went back to the hotel and he didn't come, she would only have to come back, wouldn't she? And so she might as well *do* something, mightn't she? While she was waiting for him.

Her eyes filled with tears and she brushed them impatiently away. Crying wouldn't help. Staring blindly at her sand-trails, that had been smudged by the wind, she felt despair wash over her. She'd been so *happy*. It seemed such a long time since she'd first come to the abbey, and yet it was only a few weeks. Weeks of happiness and hard work and laughter. Loving. And if the affair was over, her job over, did she just give him an invoice for work done to date?

Stopping the trembling of her lip by sheer effort

of will, she sighed. Best get on with it then, hadn't she? Until Garde came to tell her different. She would start on the paths, she decided.

She walked back to the utility room, then dragged a large bag of sand-and-cement mix out to the back, ready for re-laying the brick paving which was stacked tidily to one side.

Knife in hand, all ready to slit the bag and begin spreading it, she froze when she heard Garde's car. She felt her stomach muscles tighten, and she felt sick again.

Slowly straightening, she listened to his footsteps on the gravel, heard him speak to Sean, and then the footsteps start up again. She should have gone back to the hotel. She should have come to see him in the morning, when she was calmer, more in control. But she hadn't, and she wasn't, and so she had to face up to him. Taking a deep breath, she slowly turned.

His face was expressionless, tired—and she needed very badly to run to him, hold him tight. Only she couldn't do that, could she?

'Is that for me?' he asked quietly.

Confused, she just stared at him.

He nodded towards the lethal-looking knife in her hand, and she stared down, slowly retracted the blade and put it in her pocket. 'I came back,' she stated with soft defiance.

'So I see,' he agreed quietly. 'Are you all right?'

'Yes.' Still defiant, still feeling sick, she added, 'I don't know if I still have a job.'

'Neither do I.' His face still, his grey eyes steady, he asked, 'Where did you go?'

Looking away, she said quietly, 'Nowhere. Or nowhere I remember. I just drove for a while, then came back here.'

'Did you ever make love with him?'

Snapping back to face him, she demanded blankly, 'What?'

'You and Nick whatever-his-name-is,' he stated quietly.

'No!' she denied in shock. 'Good heavens, no! Whatever gave you that idea?'

'Because a man doesn't generally want to marry a woman without—'

'Sampling the goods?' she asked bitterly.

'No,' he said. 'Without encouragement.'

So he didn't believe her. Well, she hadn't supposed that he would, had she? 'I didn't encourage him,' she said tiredly. 'I was his *gardener*!' As I was yours. 'He didn't pay me, either.'

'And you think I won't?'

'I don't know. I don't *know*!' she repeated. 'I don't know anything. I worked for him, that was all. And every time I finished one job,' she resumed bitterly, 'and asked for my money, he would find something else for me to do. Said he would pay me at the end, give me a bonus. Some bonus. Why in God's name would he want to *marry* me?'

'Because no one else would,' he said simply.

Startled, she just stared at him.

'He thought you were stupid, malleable. His mistake.'

Not understanding, not daring to hope, she asked hesitantly, 'Why wouldn't anyone else marry him? I mean, I do know that he has a—'

'Vicious temper?'

'Yes,' she whispered.

'He's also stupid,' Garde added dismissively.

'What did you say to him? I mean, if you didn't know him—'

'I didn't. He apparently wrote to me…'

'But you don't answer unsolicited mail, do you?'

'No. And when I didn't reply, or contact him, he came down. I asked him to leave.'

'Nicely?'

He gave a small, tired smile. 'No.' Holding out his hand, he waited, and after a small hesitation she put her own into it. Was this where he told her it was finished?

'Come on. We need to talk, you and I, and I would prefer not to have an audience.'

Sean, she assumed. Well, she didn't want Sean witnessing anything, either. There had been quite enough witnessing for one day.

'I would also prefer,' he continued without inflexion as he led her towards the utility room door, 'not to have all those bushes littering my front garden. They arrived as I did.'

Halting, she peered through to the front. 'Not bushes,' she corrected. 'Your box hedging—or, to be more accurate, and just to show off, *buxus semper-*

virens "Suffruticosa".' There was no enthusiasm in her voice, just a sad emptiness.

He gave her a quick look, then tugged her through the side door. He shut it firmly behind him. Standing in the dim room, with her equipment stacked all around them, he said quietly, 'It's either the bedroom or my study.'

'Is it?'

'Yes. Depending on what sort of conversation we're going to have.'

'Formal or informal?'

'Yes.'

She could feel his breath against her face as he spoke, and she gave a small shiver. She wanted him. Wanted to be held, comforted, made love to. What did he want? Mention of the bedroom made it sound as though… 'Jen found an old magazine with a photograph of you with a top model and she—'

'Jen should mind her own business,' he stated neutrally. 'Do you know what sort of conversation you want?'

'Yes,' she whispered. 'Do you?'

'Yes. We'll use the bedroom.'

With her heart beating over-fast, because that sounded as though he wanted the same outcome as her, Sorrel gave a jerky nod and allowed him to lead her into the hall and up the stairs.

'Sit,' he ordered as he pointed to the end of the bed.

She obediently sat, her hands linked loosely in her lap, her eyes downcast.

'Ladies first,' he said softly. He didn't sound amused, just very tired.

Raising her eyes to his, she found her mind was blank. She only seemed to have feelings. 'I don't know what to say. Don't know where to start. You want me to apologise for my hysterical behaviour? Good job the reporter wasn't there—'

'Stop it,' he reproved quietly.

'Sorry. I was angry. All those months of not working because of him. All that money he owed me... He had me arrested, did I tell you that? When I refused to marry him he refused to pay me. I told him I'd take him to court—and he had me arrested. Told the police I stole some money from his house. He had the charges dropped before it could go any further. But no one *believed* me, Garde!'

'They'll believe you now,' he stated grimly.

'What?' she whispered.

'They'll believe you now,' he repeated. 'A public apology will be printed in the London papers and he will pay you what he owes. I'm sure it was him who organised the sabotage in the garden—to hurt you.'

Astonished, dumbfounded, she queried, 'But how can you make him pay?'

'I can make him.'

She believed him. Utterly.

'I don't understand you sometimes.'

'I know you don't. My fault. I couldn't afford to trust you. I wanted to, probably more than you will ever know, and so I had you investigated. I thought you might work for the press.'

'No.'

Staring down at her sad, unhappy face, a face that was meant for laughter, he added quietly, 'I'm sorry.'

'It's understandable.' Too restless to sit still, she got to her feet and went to stand by the window. 'You're a wealthy man. You only kissed me after you'd got the report, didn't you?'

'Yes.'

'Did you want to kiss me before?'

'Yes.'

Resting her hands on the sill, she stared down at her shrubs. 'And the report said that I didn't do any of the things Nick said?'

'Mmm.'

'And you believed it?'

He didn't answer immediately and she turned to look at him.

'I *wanted* to believe it. I thought you were lovers, you see—and I was jealous.'

'Jealous?'

'Yes. I didn't want you to have been with him.'

'But I hadn't.'

'No.'

'Did he say that I had?'

He hesitated a moment, then nodded. 'That's why I was angry when I followed you into the back garden. Not with you. With him, and myself. I was going to tell you earlier. I got the final report today. The PI spoke to some people who knew him—and came to his own conclusions. He didn't think you were guilty. Neither did I.'

'Why?'

He gave a wry smile. 'Mostly because I didn't want you to be, I suspect.'

'You were different, happy...'

'Yes.'

'And then Nick came.' Searching his face, his expression, she persisted, 'You really didn't believe him?'

'No.'

'Not even for a moment?'

He hesitated, before saying quietly, 'Not today, no.'

'But you did before, after you got the first report?'

'Not *believe*, but there was a niggling doubt that you *might* have been on the make,' he admitted honestly.

'And yet you still...'

'Wanted to make love to you? Yes. You weren't entirely sure of me either, were you?'

'No. Because of Jen, because she says I have screwed judgement—and because maybe, just maybe, I have. I don't want to be like this, suspicious of people, waiting for the cracks to show, for someone to change...'

'No,' he agreed. 'Not very nice, is it?'

'No.'

'Did you really think I wouldn't pay you?'

She shook her head.

'Sorrel,' he warned.

'I didn't. Well, not until today, anyway. And you are famous after all, aren't you?'

'No... Well, yes, I suppose,' he said gently. 'I was well-photographed. I made a lot of money fairly quickly, was invited here, there, everywhere... It was a lifestyle that soon palled.'

'What was she like?' she asked casually. Too casually.

'Who?'

'The model. Serena someone...'

'Verena,' he corrected. 'She was actually quite nice, but we weren't lovers, if that's what you're asking. I like to do my loving in private, not under full media attention.'

'You also lied to me, didn't you?'

Still gentle, still being very careful of her feelings, he asked, 'Did I? When?'

'When you said why you were grumpy, that first day we met. It wasn't because of Mrs Davies or the ramblers, was it?'

He smiled. 'No. The press had just found out something I didn't want them to know.'

She waited.

He gave a soft laugh as he watched some of the animation return to her face. 'Nothing nefarious,' he assured her. 'I gave some money to charity, that's all.'

'A lot of money?' she guessed.

'Mmm, enough to fund a motor neurone unit. My grandfather died of the disease.'

'Oh!' she exclaimed inadequately. 'Not your father?'

'No. He died in his sleep a few years ago. My

mother died when I was born. Anything else you
want to know?'

She shook her head.

'Have we talked enough, do you suppose?'

'I don't know,' she said helplessly.

'Are you still angry?'

'With Nick?'

'No, with me.'

She gave a little shake of her head. 'I wasn't angry
with you.'

'Not even because I mistrusted you?'

'No, because we both did the same, didn't we?
Shut it away because—'

'We wanted each other?'

'Yes, and because I was afraid of being hurt—'

'Or made to look a fool?'

'Yes. So what happens now?'

'We have a relationship,' he said carefully. 'A
proper relationship.'

Startled out of her introspection, she asked worriedly, 'What's a proper relationship?'

'Sharing, caring, trusting. Just in case you hadn't
noticed,' he added wryly, 'I fell in love with you.'

'When?'

He gave a small, abrupt laugh. 'I don't know. I
only know that I've been hating myself for not trusting you, that I've been driving round the countryside
looking for you, out of my mind with worry...'

'Have you?' she asked in astonishment. 'Is that
where you went?'

'Mmm. I heard you leave, so I dumped the cupboard on the floor to run after you—but by the time I'd got my car out of the garage you were long gone. You don't want a loving relationship?'

'Yes. No. Oh, I don't know!' she wailed. Yes, she did. She *did* want it, but... 'But you're *famous*!'

'And you don't know why everyone wants to marry you?'

'*Marry?*' she asked hoarsely. 'You didn't say *marry*!'

'No, but it's what I'd like.'

'But *why?*'

'Because you're nice to have around?'

'Oh, well, that's a really good reason, isn't it? I don't know that I *want* to get married.'

'I know. I was hoping to persuade you.' Holding out one hand, he waggled his fingers.

Ignoring it, she continued to stare at him in worry.

'I'm thirty-seven,' he said, almost conversationally.

'What's that got to do with anything?'

'I want a family.'

Her stomach dipped and she turned hastily back to the window. 'Adopt,' she said. She'd meant to sound flippant, only it came out as a croak.

'Don't you want my babies, Sorrel?'

'No,' she denied weakly. His *babies*? They barely knew each other.

'I could keep you in the style to which you'd like to become accustomed.'

'You don't know what I'd like.'

'But I want to.'

Slamming her hands on the windowsill, she cried, 'I never gave you any reason to suppose I wanted marriage. Never, ever did I say I expected anything.'

'True.'

'Then *why*?'

'Don't you like me?' he asked instead.

'You know very well I like you!'

'Then marry me.'

'No.'

'Cruel lady,' he mocked softly. 'And just when I'd found someone I wanted to rub oil on my back.'

'You don't really love me,' she blurted.

Covering the short distance between them, he turned her to face him. Tilting up her chin, he stared down into her eyes. 'I just told you that I do.'

Lowering her lashes, she mumbled, 'You didn't mean it.' Staring down at her hands, she saw they were covered in cement dust and hastily shoved them behind her back.

'And you don't think you could come to love me?'

Refusing to look up, she didn't answer.

'Is it the money that puts you off?' he asked kindly.

She shook her head. 'I'm not intimidated by money—probably because I've never had any,' she muttered. 'Neither am I impressed by it. So don't use that as a lever.'

'No,' he agreed, 'but desperate plights call for desperate measures. What about if I gave all my money away?'

Diverted, she looked up. 'Don't be so ridic—'

Breaking off, because the expression on his face was so—loving, she swallowed hard, felt tears form in her eyes. 'How can you be sure you love me?'

'I don't know,' he said gently. 'I only know that I would die for you; that you excite me and amuse me; that just a glimpse of you makes me smile. I feel protective and proud...' Gently smoothing her unruly hair back, he rested his thumbs against her cheek bones. 'I waited a long time to meet you, and then I couldn't trust—and it hurt, Sorrel, because I wanted so very much to love. To share, to be a part of something again. To have children, a normal life. When I couldn't find you, when no one I asked had seen your battered old truck, I worried about you. You were all upset...'

'And dirty,' she put in.

'And dirty,' he agreed with a small smile. '*Very* dirty, but then, I like you dirty. I'd watch you from the windows sometimes and I'd want to join you, hold you. Hair all untidy, sweaty, grubby—you always looked so contented, happy, like a child. I don't know why I love you—don't even really know what love is—I only know that I don't want to lose you, that you make me feel whole.'

'Belonging,' she said softly.

'Yes.'

Closing her eyes, she rested her forehead against his chest. 'I've felt like that since the first time we made love. As though I belonged. But we haven't known each other very long, and it's such a big step, marriage.'

'But you're very brave. We don't need to have a family straight away, if that's what frightens you.' Smoothing his thumbs to her jaw and back again, he added, 'I've never met anyone like you, and doubt I ever will again. I wanted very badly to laugh when you first came into my house, took over. But I couldn't afford to, just in case. I want to introduce you to my friends…'

'You do have friends, then? I was beginning to wonder when you continually refused to answer your phone,' she murmured softly, almost absently, as she stared into his eyes. Amazing eyes, fantastic eyes, eyes she wanted to brush her mouth over. A face she wanted desperately to kiss. A body she wanted desperately to hold.

His voice was as absent as hers, and his eyes sent messages that made her feel blurred, achy. 'I only refused to answer it when *you* were there. When we came back from rescuing the dog, and when you came the next day, I switched off the answering machine. Not knowing who you were, I didn't want you to overhear anything. Anyway, my friends are leaving me alone while I—rusticate.'

Voice barely audible, her body melted towards his. 'And when you've stopped rusticating, what then?'

'I don't know. Might be fun to find out, mightn't it? You could still do your gardens. And you're very good at ignoring reporters, aren't you? I won't say your lifestyle won't change, but I don't think you're the sort of person to want to drag me to parties, dinners, shopping, are you?'

'No. Don't you like that sort of thing?'

'No. When I eventually start working again, find something I want to do, I want to be able to come home at night, know you'll be there to tease me, make me laugh, put everything into perspective. Does that sound boring to you? Chauvinistic?'

She shook her head.

'Then will you?'

Would she? 'I don't know,' she whispered. 'How can I think when I want you so badly?'

He groaned and bent to capture her mouth. He savoured the soft fullness of her lips beneath his and wanted her with a desperation that might have astonished him a few weeks previously. He could barely remember a life when he hadn't known her, wanted her. He slid his arms round her, held her against him with warm persuasion, until the kiss deepened, became more urgent, and so very necessary. He touched every part of her he could reach, compulsively, gently, a roving exploration that made her shiver against him.

Her own hands were clutching his back, his arms, his sides, and her breathing was coming in funny little gasps as his mouth sought hers again and again, and again.

'I don't intend to ever let you go, Sorrel,' he warned thickly against her mouth.

'No,' she agreed, her voice as husky as his. 'Don't ever let me go.'

CHAPTER NINE

THEY were married in September.

She'd spent her last night as Miss James in the small hotel she'd stayed in previously. Jen was there, and her husband Giles, who was to give her away, and the naughty one, who was to be page boy, and under strict instructions not to get dirty.

'Nervous?' Jen whispered as she straightened Sorrel's veil for at least the fifth time as they waited for the car to arrive.

'No,' Sorrel denied softly as she picked up the small bouquet of roses cut from the abbey garden less than half an hour before.

'I am,' Jen confessed.

'I know.' Sorrel smiled.

'I can't believe that you're going to marry someone so, well...'

'Special?'

'Wealthy,' Jen corrected.

'Wealth doesn't matter,' Sorrel said. 'It's *nice*—' she grinned '—but it doesn't matter.'

'No,' Jen agreed drily. 'You'd live with him on a desert island without any mod cons, wouldn't you? If he asked. I don't think I've ever seen two people who so consistently can't keep their hands off each other.'

'Making up for lost time,' Sorrel murmured. And it was true. Ever since the day Nick had come things had been different. Knowing that Garde loved her, knowing how *much* he loved her—which still seemed somewhat incomprehensible—things had been different. Decadent. There was *nothing* they couldn't do to each other, say to each other…

'Why are you smiling?' Jen asked softly.

'Oh, just thinking.' Giving her sister a sideways glance, Sorrel giggled.

'I love you, big sister,' Jen said softly.

A sudden lump in her throat, Sorrel nodded and swallowed hard. 'I know. I love you too.'

'And I feel almost—jealous. Isn't that silly? Ever since Mum and Dad died, I've felt I've sort of had to look after you. And now…' Jen gave a hasty sniff, a wobbly smile. 'Don't take any notice. I'm just being emotional. God, I hope I don't cry.'

'The cars are here,' Giles announced as he walked in from outside, carrying his son. He gave his wife a searching glance, a wry smile, and looked at Sorrel. 'She's going to cry,' he announced.

'Yep,' Sorrel agreed. They grinned at each other.

'And you look lovely. Like a stork,' he teased, 'but lovely. He's a lucky man.'

'Thank you.'

'And there's an army of reporters outside.'

'Oh b—'

'Don't say it!' he warned quickly as he glanced at his son. A son who was being entirely too quiet, which didn't bode well. 'Little pitchers and all that...' He handed the little rascal to his wife, and, waiting for them to leave first, he held out his arm for Sorrel to take. 'Thank you for asking me to give you away,' he whispered softly. 'It's an honour.'

'Thank you for accepting.' And suddenly, now, she felt tearful. This was her family. The only family she had.

'I was always afraid,' he confessed as he led her carefully down the front steps, 'that I wouldn't like your choice of man. But I do. Very much. And so I can give you into his care with a good heart.'

'He is nice, isn't he?' Sorrel asked naively.

'Yes.'

She blinked as a whole raft of camera flashes went off, and quickly climbed into the car for the short journey to the abbey. It had been her choice for the wedding to take place at his home. It was what she wanted. And Garde hadn't let her near the place for the past week. Goodness only knew what he'd been doing. The kitchen was finished; she'd finished the front and rear gardens; a small downstairs cloakroom had been installed and the refectory had been cleaned until it shone. Mrs Davies had been inspired—but she wasn't staying. Her husband had found a job in Bristol and they were moving to the city.

And Sorrel was getting married.

Suddenly, it was real.

In a little under an hour she would be Mrs Chevenay.

She took a deep breath, that severely strained the

tiny buttons that ran down the front of her long off-white dress, then slowly let it out.

'All right?' Giles asked softly.

She nodded and stared out at the woods where she had parked that day in order to catch a vandal, and she smiled. Turning her head, she watched the garden come into view. It no longer looked new, but as though it had always been like that, and she was pleased, and then startled, as the cavalcade of reporters roared past them and halted just beyond the bridge.

She stared, glanced at Giles, and burst out laughing. She hoped their official photographer was among that lot, but even if he wasn't it wouldn't spoil it. Nothing was going to spoil her day. The sun was shining, birds were singing, and she saw a great many cars were parked on her new gravel drive.

And, inside, Garde would be waiting. Was he nervous? she wondered. No, she didn't think he would be.

The front doors stood open with no one to be seen. The car halted, and as Giles helped her out a lone photographer walked down the drive and asked her to pose. Which she did.

He also followed them inside, and their feet echoed on the polished tiles as they walked slowly towards the refectory. As they reached the door, it silently opened. Framed in the doorway, she stared round her in wonder. To her right, there were row upon row of gilt chairs, all full with their guests.

Pictures adorned the once stark walls. Flowers filled the fireplace and several stands around the room.

To her left stood a grand piano, being played by an unknown gentleman in white tie and tails. Moving her gaze further on, feeling dazed, unreal, she watched filmy white curtains blow gently in the breeze from the open French doors that looked out onto her newly laid garden. The minister stood there, watching her, waiting, and in front of him Garde, with his best man. Garde was also watching her; and now she had eyes only for him.

He smiled. A warm, generous, open, teasing smile, and she smiled back. And then she laughed, an infectious, wholly delightful laugh, and ran to him.

He caught her up, hugged her, and smiled down into her happy face. 'Hello.'

'Hello,' she echoed, and rubbed her nose softly against his.

There was gentle laughter from the guests and the minister cleared his throat, ready to begin.

Stepping back, eyes alight with mischief, she turned to hand her bouquet to the naughty one—who was utterly refusing to be handed *anything*. Face mutinous, hands behind his back, her two-year-old nephew stared at her as though she had betrayed him. Perhaps she had. Giles took the flowers instead, his face creased with amusement. Jen hastily got up to take them from him.

'Dearly beloved...'

A small body squirmed between herself and Garde and announced loudly, 'Choclit!'

Everyone dissolved into laughter, including the minister, and a red-faced Jen hastily removed her son from the proceedings.

Half an hour later, Garde was invited to kiss the bride. He did so with a great deal of enthusiasm. Photographs were taken—and not only by the official photographer. Because as Garde led his new wife out onto the terrace, the bevy of press photographers snapped away quickly before hastily dispersing. And then she saw the marquee. A very large, very white marquee that had been set up where the old green-houses had once stood.

'I've been busy,' he said softly. 'And I want you to myself. Now. Immediately. I love you.' Searching her face, taking in everything there was to take in about this girl he didn't think he could live without, he added quietly, 'I'd never said that to anyone be-fore, and now I don't want to stop saying it.' Oblivious of the people milling round them, admiring the garden, making their way to the marquee, he kissed her, so very, very, gently, almost reverently, on the mouth.

Her heart full, she whispered, 'I love you too. I'd *die* for you.' Touching her fingers to his face, his mouth, she added, 'You said that once, to me.' With a sudden radiant smile, she hugged him tight. 'But not today. Today is for living.'

'And loving.'

'Yes. Where are we going afterwards?' she asked quickly, hoping to catch him out, as she'd been hop-ing to catch him out for weeks.

'It's a secret. But I will tell you one thing,' he teased as he captured her hand and led her towards the marquee.

'What's that?'

'There won't be any people there.'

'Sounds good.'

'It will be. Do those fancy buttons undo?' he asked interestedly as he took a glass of champagne from the waiter at the entrance to the marquee and handed it to her.

'Mmm,' she agreed with a little smile.

He took his own glass and toasted her. 'To my wife.' His eyes were warm, and exciting, and full of promise.

It's hard to resist the lure of the
Australian Outback

One of Harlequin Romance's
best-loved Australian authors

Margaret Way

brings you

Legends of the **OUTBACK**

Look for

A WIFE AT KIMBARA (#3595)
March 2000

THE BRIDESMAID'S WEDDING (#3607)
June 2000

THE ENGLISH BRIDE (#3619)
September 2000

Available at your favorite retail outlet.

HARLEQUIN®
Makes any time special.™

Visit us at www.romance.net   HROUT

NEARLYWEDS

**Almost at the altar—
will these *nearly*weds
become *newly*weds?**

Harlequin Romance® is delighted to invite
you to some special weddings! Yet these are
no ordinary weddings. Our beautiful brides
and gorgeous grooms only *nearly* make it
to the altar—before fate intervenes.

But the story doesn't end there....
Find out what happens in these
tantalizingly emotional novels!

Authors to look out for include:

**Leigh Michaels—The Bridal Swap
Liz Fielding—His Runaway Bride
Janelle Denison—The Wedding Secret
Renee Roszel—Finally a Groom
Caroline Anderson—The Impetuous Bride**

Available wherever Harlequin books are sold.

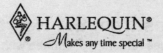

HARLEQUIN®
Makes any time special ™

Visit us at www.eHarlequin.com   HRNEAR

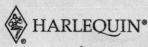 **HARLEQUIN®**

makes any time special—online...

eHARLEQUIN.com

your romantic life

—Romance 101—
❤ Guides to romance, dating and flirting.

—Dr. Romance —
❤ Get romance advice and tips from
our expert, Dr. Romance.

—Recipes for Romance—
❤ How to plan romantic meals for you
and your sweetie.

—Daily Love Dose—
❤ Tips on how to keep the romance
alive every day.

—Tales from the Heart—
❤ Discuss romantic dilemmas with other
members in our Tales from the Heart
message board.

HINTL1

If you enjoyed what you just read,
then we've got an offer you can't resist!

Take 2 bestselling love stories FREE!
Plus get a FREE surprise gift!

Clip this page and mail it to Harlequin Reader Service®

IN U.S.A.
3010 Walden Ave.
P.O. Box 1867
Buffalo, N.Y. 14240-1867

IN CANADA
P.O. Box 609
Fort Erie, Ontario
L2A 5X3

YES! Please send me 2 free Harlequin Romance® novels and my free surprise gift. Then send me 6 brand-new novels every month, which I will receive months before they're available in stores. In the U.S.A., bill me at the bargain price of $2.90 plus 25¢ delivery per book and applicable sales tax, if any*. In Canada, bill me at the bargain price of $3.34 plus 25¢ delivery per book and applicable taxes**. That's the complete price and a savings of 10% off the cover prices—what a great deal! I understand that accepting the 2 free books and gift places me under no obligation ever to buy any books. I can always return a shipment and cancel at any time. Even if I never buy another book from Harlequin, the 2 free books and gift are mine to keep forever. So why not take us up on our invitation. You'll be glad you did!

186 HEN C4GY
386 HEN C4GZ

Name	(PLEASE PRINT)	
Address	Apt.#	
City	State/Prov.	Zip/Postal Code

* Terms and prices subject to change without notice. Sales tax applicable in N.Y.
** Canadian residents will be charged applicable provincial taxes and GST.
All orders subject to approval. Offer limited to one per household.
® are registered trademarks of Harlequin Enterprises Limited.

HROM00_R2   ©1998 Harlequin Enterprises Limited

Harlequin proudly brings you

STELLA CAMERON
Bobby Hutchinson
Sandra Marton

in

MARRIED IN SPRING

a brand-new anthology in which three couples find that when spring arrives, romance soon follows…along with an unexpected walk down the aisle!

February 2001

Available wherever Harlequin books are sold.

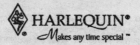

HARLEQUIN®
Makes any time special ™

Visit us at www.eHarlequin.com

PHMARRIED

In March 2001,

Silhouette Desire

presents the next book in

DIANA PALMER's

enthralling *Soldiers of Fortune* trilogy:

THE WINTER SOLDIER

Cy Parks had a reputation around Jacobsville for his taciturn and solitary ways. But spirited Lisa Monroe wasn't put off by the mesmerizing mercenary, and drove him to distraction with her sweetly tantalizing kisses. Though he'd never admit it, Cy was getting mighty possessive of the enchanting woman who needed the type of safeguarding only he could provide. But who would protect the beguiling beauty from *him...?*

Soldiers of Fortune...prisoners of love.

Silhouette®
Where love comes alive™

Available only from Silhouette Desire at your favorite retail outlet.

Visit Silhouette at
www.eHarlequin.com

SDWS

#1 *New York Times* bestselling author

NORA ROBERTS

**brings you more of the loyal and loving,
tempestuous and tantalizing Stanislaski family.**

Coming in February 2001

The Stanislaski Sisters

Natasha and Rachel

Though raised in the Old World traditions of their
family, fiery Natasha Stanislaski and cool, classy
Rachel Stanislaski are ready for a *new* world of love....

*And also available in February 2001 from
Silhouette Special Edition, the newest book in the
heartwarming Stanislaski saga*

CONSIDERING KATE

Natasha and Spencer Kimball's daughter Kate turns her
back on old dreams and returns to her hometown, where
she finds the *man* of her dreams.

Available at your favorite retail outlet.

Where love comes alive™

Visit Silhouette at www.eHarlequin.com   PSSTANSIS